A Sunshine Christmas

THE SUNSHINE SERIES
BOOK FOUR

LILLY MIRREN

Chapter One

Maree Houston was sick and tired of moving house. She'd lived in so many places over the past five years that she barely had time to pack before she was onto the next place. And with the rising cost of living, she was struggling to pay rent on her own with her four-year-old, Sam. That's why she'd finally asked Jemma if they could move in with her and Dan. They had a cute little two-bedroom apartment across the road from the beach. Jemma agreed—they were trying to save up to have a baby and could use the rent money. And so, Maree and Sam had moved into the small guest room. It was like a huge weight had been lifted from Maree's shoulders, and she finally felt as though she could breathe.

She wandered out onto the cozy balcony that jutted over the communal swimming pool and tented a hand over her eyes to cut the glare of the afternoon sun. It'd been five years since her divorce, and she'd struggled to find her footing ever since. She'd lived in Sunshine all of her life, but it felt strange now. As though she didn't quite belong.

Everyone in Sunshine knew about her and Jack. They'd both grown up in the small seaside hamlet on Bribie Island, attended local schools and worked in local businesses. Jack still had family on the island, although he'd moved away after their divorce. Her own family was gone—her parents had passed, and the rest of her family lived on the mainland. Her friends in Sunshine were the only real family she had left—and Sam. He was her all. Her whole world revolved around him. Sometimes it felt as though she'd given up on everything but him.

She turned back into the apartment and tied an apron neatly around her waist over the top of her white blouse and long black pants. Then she went to the bathroom and cleaned her teeth, fixed her hair into a tidy bun at the nape of her neck. Sam was already at daycare. It was time to go to work.

The drive to the Aurora Boutique Inn and Bistro was only three minutes. She'd timed it the first day after moving in with Jemma and Dan.

Gwen had hired her a few months earlier, and so far, she'd enjoyed the work. She was a waitress and sometimes bartender in the bistro. The hours suited her study schedule, and the pay was decent.

She was studying online to become a financial planner. But at the rate she was going, she'd finally graduate and start working right before retirement. At least, it often felt that way.

The restaurant was already busy when she arrived. The evening shift always was. She clocked in and hurried to the kitchen to get the update on specials from the chef.

"You're early, nice to see," Anthony said. He wore a white double-breasted shirt, long black pants, and a white hat that covered his dark, wavy hair. His brown eyes twinkled at her. "The specials today are a lamb shank navarin with turnips and carrots, along with a crusty sourdough bread straight out of the oven. Then we have a fresh-caught barramundi encrusted with breadcrumbs and macadamia alongside a double-cream mashed potato and mixed greens. And finally, the soup of the day is a seafood bisque featuring Moreton Bay Bugs."

She wrote notes in a small notebook she kept in her pocket. "Those sound delicious." Her stomach grumbled. She was hungry already and hadn't started her shift yet. By the end of the shift, she was always ravenous and couldn't wait to eat whatever the chef had left for the staff. The previous evening, she'd polished off a dish of boeuf bourguignon, and it was so delicious, she'd eaten until she was completely stuffed full.

"Don't forget, we're also offering mulled wine for the Christmas holiday season. And there's a French Cotillion Christmas chocolate cake with whipped cream for dessert."

She gave a nod. "Got it. I'm going to die of hunger before this shift is over."

He dipped his head in the direction of the stove. "Grab yourself a breadstick before you get started. They're hot out of the oven."

"Thank you, Chef!" she said with a grin as she hurried to fetch one.

She carried it out of the way and slathered it with butter, then sat on a stool to eat while she waited for her shift to start. It would stave off her hunger for the first couple of hours. She was glad to be at work. She liked to be busy, and the dinner shift only got more hectic with each passing minute. By seven o'clock, it was in full swing. She was run off her feet, taking orders, delivering meals and clearing tables.

The lamb shanks were a big hit with at least one person at every table ordering them. They looked succulent and smelled divine. The meat was falling off the bone, and she hoped the chef would set some aside for the staff, although it wasn't likely given how popular they were.

She carried four plates of lamb shanks to a table. The plates were hot on her arms and hands. She set them down with relief and a smile, and then hurried to the next table, where the hostess had seated another five people.

She stopped short, her heart in her throat. She recognised them all.

"Hi, Maree," the woman said, her chestnut hair perfectly groomed into a bob, her grey eyes highlighted by elegant brown eyeshadow. "I didn't expect to see you here."

"Hello, Margaret. How lovely to run into you all like this."

She glanced across the table to see her ex-husband, Jack, staring at her with wide grey eyes, so like his mother's.

"Jack, it's good to see you too."

He nodded, his cheeks colouring. "Hello, Maree."

It was awkward. There was no way around that. It was the first time she'd seen Jack with his entire family since the divorce five years earlier. His father, Tom, stared at her then glanced down at his menu with a cough to clear his throat. His sister, Meg, smiled shyly at Maree. They'd always gotten on well, and she had been sad when they lost touch.

She pulled her notepad from her pocket. She was going to need to write down this order—there was no way she'd be able to remember a thing. Her head felt light, and she thought she might need to sit down. But she'd take the order first. She didn't want them to see her upset.

"You're working here?" Jack asked.

She swallowed. "That's right. I've been here for a few months now. Gwen—that's the owner—is a friend of a friend. She gave me a chance, and so far, I'm loving it." She was waffling. That's what she did when she was nervous. She always suffered from verbal diahorrea when she felt anxious. And the worst part was that Jack knew it.

His eyes crinkled around the edges. "That's good. Are you full time?"

"No, only part time. I'm studying," she replied. "Are you here for a holiday?"

Jack glanced at his mother, then his father. He inhaled a sharp breath. "Actually, I moved back. Dad retired, and I'm staying with them for a while, spending some time ... you know, catching up."

"I didn't retire. I cut back," his father corrected him in a gruff voice. "I can do my work from anywhere."

"Right, of course. That's what I meant," Jack said.

"Oh," was all Maree could think to say. He was back? But Sunshine was her home, not his. She didn't want him here. He'd been gone for five years. What would she do now? She couldn't run into him around every corner. It would drive her crazy. She'd survived the past five years by never seeing him.

"I'm sure we'll run into each other," he said as if reading her thoughts.

She forced a smile onto her face. "I'm sure we will. So, what can I get you?"

She wrote down their orders and then rushed back to the kitchen. Leaning against the counter as she tried her best to catch her breath, she fought hard to keep the tears at bay. Jack was back in Sunshine. He was living here. She couldn't wrap her head around it. When he'd left, she never thought she'd see him again. And now, he was here, in her restaurant, living in her town.

"You okay, honey?" another waitress asked, concern etched on her face.

Maree placed the order with a nod. "Fine, thanks."

She turned on her heel and fled back out through the restaurant and onto the back deck. It was closed for dinner this evening, so she had the space to herself. Decorated with lights, it looked romantic and cozy in the warm evening air. Stars twinkled overhead. She leaned against the railing and took deep, gulping breaths. Tears filled her eyes. She brushed them away with the heel of her hand as her heart rate slowly returned to its normal pace.

"You okay?" Jack's voice startled her, sending her heart into a frenzy again.

She spun to face him. "Uh, yeah, I'm fine."

"I know it's weird to run into me like this. We haven't seen each other in so long..." He slowly walked closer.

"Five years, four months, three days ... but who's counting?"

He chuckled. "Wow, that's very specific."

"I live here. This is my hometown."

He leaned against the railing beside her, arms folded over his chest. "I know. It used to be my home too. And now it is again."

"Why?" she asked, looking up at him.

"Mum and Dad wanted me to move back. They're getting older, and I don't see them as often as they would like. Plus, a few months with them has given me a chance to save for a house."

"Oh? Where will you buy?"

"Haven't decided yet. But I'm setting up my practice in Sunshine, so I might settle here."

He was a physiotherapist. He'd always been so smart. She'd worked hard to put him through university. He was supposed to return the favour, but they'd separated right after his graduation. They'd married young. Too young, really. Everyone had warned her—they should wait, they shouldn't rush into it, there was plenty of time—but they hadn't listened.

"I don't know if I can..." She didn't want to finish the sentence, wouldn't give him the satisfaction of knowing how much he'd rattled her.

"It'll be fine. It's been five years. We'll be friends. I've missed you." His eyes narrowed. "We can manage it, can't we?"

She chewed on her lower lip, then gave a quick nod. "Of course. Friends—I can do that."

"We should hang out. It'll give us a chance to put things

behind us and move on. You know, so there's no awkwardness."

"We're definitely not there yet," she agreed.

He laughed. "It's very awkward right now."

"I'm glad it's not just me." She laughed along with him.

"So, we'll hang out?"

"Okay, sure. Why not?"

Chapter Two

Christmas carols floated through the living room as Jemma Grant draped colourful lights around her Christmas tree. The plastic tree was a deep shade of green, and she'd placed a red-and-gold skirt around the bottom. It looked pretty, and she was happy with how it was coming together. It was early, but she didn't care. She'd waited as long as she could to decorate. It might help her feel more at peace with the world.

It was their second year in this flat. Last Christmas, they'd decorated a house plant, but this year she'd splurged and bought a Christmas tree along with a boatload of decorations. It was probably a bit too much for the small space, but it made her feel cozy, and that was exactly what she needed right now.

She turned the carols up with a tap to her phone, then leaned back against the sofa to survey her work. Hmm ... it needed more gold. There was too much red and not enough sparkle.

She reached into the box on the floor by her elbow and pulled out the first ornament she touched. She held it up to the light, turning it over and over to study it.

Baby's first Christmas.

She shouldn't have bought it. She knew that now. It was premature. The ornament, not the baby. She'd never had a pregnancy last more than a few weeks so far. They'd been trying for a baby for years now. It felt like forever, although it'd probably been no more than two. They'd been married three. And although they hadn't really done much to prevent getting pregnant that first year, they hadn't actively tried. So, it didn't really count.

With a sigh, she placed the ornament back in the box, and then pulled out another one. This was a reindeer with a sleigh attached. It was colourful and made of porcelain, and she loved this ornament. It reminded her of their honeymoon at Whistler Ski Resort. They'd had such a wonderful time. She'd loved the winter wonderland—snow everywhere, skiing for days. It'd been a dream come true. They'd been so much in love.

These days, the romance was tempered by the fact that there was no baby in the second bedroom. Instead, she'd allowed her friend, Maree, to move into the room with her son, Sam. Much to Dan's dismay.

"I thought we were trying for a baby," he'd hissed when Maree was unpacking her things.

"We are."

He dipped his head in Maree's direction. "Where will we put it if they're in the spare room?"

Jemma had sighed. "I'm sure we've got time to help her find somewhere else. And besides, a baby doesn't take up much room when it arrives. We can use a bassinet." She did her best to sound positive, but inside she felt a stabbing pain as though she might burst into tears at that very moment. Because the truth was, she'd almost given up hope at this point. Maree might as well move in since they weren't likely to get pregnant. The doctor has said as much when he called her womb hostile. As though there were warriors with spears, fighting to keep all the babies at bay.

She liked to think of it that way because at least she could laugh through the tears at her own silly imagination.

Jemma stood with a grunt and pushed the reindeer ornament onto a branch, and then stepped back, head tipped to one side to check that it was in the perfect spot, at the right angle. And it was.

The heat was unbearable today, and she had to switch on the air-conditioning to help stop her from sweating so profusely. And it also fit better with the words to the songs about white Christmases, sleigh bells ringing, and chestnuts roasting on an open fire.

The only thing roasting in this flat was her.

She went to turn the fan on just as Dan opened the front door.

"I'm home!" he called.

"Hi, honey," she said.

He came over to give her a kiss, but it was on her cheek rather than her lips. She'd felt as though he was pulling away from her recently. Maybe she was overly sensitive or imagining things, but there was a tension between the two of them she couldn't quite understand.

"How was your day?" she asked as she pulled a strand of tinsel out of the Christmas box.

He filled a glass with water in the kitchen, then wandered back into the living room as he gulped it down. "It was fine, I guess. I'm overloaded on human interaction, though. Movie tonight?"

She nodded. "Sounds good. I'm ovulating... at least I think I am. I'm so irregular who can say. But according to the calendar it should be sometime soon."

His nostrils flared, but he didn't say anything. He took

another swig of water. "You know I don't like the pressure. Plus, I'm not feeling up to it tonight."

It'd made both of them feel like a couple of breeding cattle recently. All they ever talked about was work or getting pregnant. Or what they might do if it didn't work—adopt or foster ... she'd seen how much he'd begun to tense up whenever she raised the subject, and yet couldn't seem to stop herself. She wanted a baby so badly.

"I understand," she said, although she felt frustrated with him. She only ovulated once per month. The least he could do was his part. It wasn't such a big ask. But she held her tongue. Instead, she said, "Want to help me decorate the tree?"

"Not really. Sorry, I'm tired. I thought I might go for a surf before the sun goes down. Don't want to be a shark's dinner."

"Speaking of dinner, anything you'd like?"

"How about steak?"

"Sounds perfect. Do you want to pick some up on your way home?"

"Sure, that's fine."

He changed into a wetsuit and left to surf at Sunshine Beach while Jemma finished up with the decorating. In previous years, they'd decorated together. They'd sipped mulled wine or eggnog and hung ornaments and lights while chattering and laughing over their plans and dreams for the year ahead. When he walked out, surfboard beneath his arm, it was like a punch to the gut for her. He didn't want to stay and spend time with her. He seemed to prefer his own company most of the time these days. Would their marriage survive their infertility? She didn't know.

If only she could fall pregnant. Having a baby would change everything. The two of them would finally be happy. They'd have the joy they'd been missing back in their lives. They'd find that first love again, she was sure of it. The stress and strain of trying to get pregnant had shaken their relationship, but it was something they could resurrect. A baby was all they needed to repair the cracks in their marriage. If only she could do something about it. But she was powerless to make this one thing happen, and it pained her more than she could say.

Chapter Three

The sun had risen and hung hot and bright over the dark ocean. Maree stood with her wetsuit half-shucked to her waist. She held a hand over her eyes to shield them from the glare of the sun and studied the break. It was smooth today with the waves curling perfectly to shore. There was no wind, so the surface rose and fell gently, even with somewhat larger than usual swells. She thought about Sam, still snug in his bed back at home in the unit. Jemma had promised to feed him breakfast when he woke. Maree missed him already, the scent of his little face as he pushed it up against hers beneath the covers, saying, "Morning, Mummy. I'm hungry."

Beside her, Jack put on a layer of suncream. "You ready to go out?"

"I haven't surfed in a while. The water is always so cold at this time of day."

"It's not cold at all. You'll be used to it in thirty seconds."

"You always say that," she replied with a smile.

The two of them had run into each other again at the grocery store, and Jack had suggested an early morning surf like they used to do when they were married. She'd wondered

15

if it was too much—the nostalgia might be more painful than she was willing to bear. But he'd looked so hopeful, she couldn't turn him down. He'd always had those puppy-dog eyes that she couldn't resist. She wondered again, for the hundredth time, how she'd ever managed to divorce him.

But they'd done the right thing, hadn't they? They were too young, too different. They wanted very different things from life. And from each other. She couldn't be the person he wanted her to be, and he'd been in a bad place—grieving. Now she found it hard to remember what it was that had driven him away. Was it her? Or was he simply unable to cope with the loss of his twin brother?

She'd had a lot of therapy since the divorce, dealt with the trauma from her childhood that she'd never had the guts to face before. It'd helped her to see herself and the world through new eyes. She'd been so angry with him, but deep down, she'd blamed herself.

He was the bad guy—he broke their vows and left. But it seemed obvious to her that the reason was her own inadequacies—she'd never been much good at intimacy or communication. She'd never had the kind of family that taught her healthy ways to do those things. Her therapist had shown her that she was worthy of love and not doomed to be alone forever. There was nothing intrinsically wrong with her. Their marriage simply hadn't worked out.

Maybe he wasn't the villain she'd thought him to be either. And she was grateful he was back, now that the initial shock had passed. It gave her a chance to really find some closure and to move past the painful rock in her chest that'd been her companion ever since he walked out of their flat on that dreadful day.

"Okay, you're right. I get used to it, and then I love it. I should do this more often. Although I probably won't manage a wave today since I haven't done it in so long."

"It's like riding a bike," he said with a grin that made her heart skip a beat. He pulled his wetsuit over his shoulders and used the string to zip it up in the back. He lifted his surfboard beneath his arm and jogged down to the water's edge.

With quick glance at the sky where clouds were threatening, she did the same, following in his footsteps.

The water was cold. It made her gasp for air as soon as it passed her chest. But then she was in, on her board, and paddling towards a wave. She duck-dived beneath it, then rose on the other side with a shake of her head that sent droplets of water flying in every direction. Paddling again, she smiled to herself. The water was already warm and felt good. Everything about this felt good.

Jack caught the first wave before she'd even reached the back of the swell. She sat on her board, feet dangling, and watched. He landed with a splash that made her laugh. She waited for him to paddle back out to her again. His golden curls were askew, his tanned face full of happiness.

"That was amazing. It's so good to be back home. I've missed this place. And..." He stopped, swallowed, and looked away.

Was he going to say he'd missed her as well? He'd mentioned that at the inn when they'd spoken on the back porch. She hadn't thought she'd ever hear him speak to her that way since the divorce. He'd been so angry when he left. Or maybe it was another emotion she hadn't fully recognised, that looked like anger when it took hold of him.

But he'd changed. So had she. They were both older. Maybe he'd worked through his issues the same way she had. Not that he had as many as her. He'd come from a healthy, happy family, and her attachment issues had been something of a shock to him. He was young and inexperienced; he didn't know how to deal with her pain or the way she pushed him away.

It was hard for her to say the words. "I'm glad you're back."

He flashed her a grateful smile. "Me too."

"I'm sorry about how everything went between us…"

"So am I."

She felt a warmth wash over her soul. She'd been so nervous about coming surfing with him today. Worried he'd make her feel even worse about herself and the choices she'd made over the years. That he'd blame her for their marriage breaking down. But of course, he didn't do that. It wasn't him —he was a good man. Always had been. If only she'd been able to recognise that when they were in the middle of the worst of it. He'd reacted badly to her. She'd responded in even worse ways to him, confident that he'd reject her at some point anyway, so she might as well get in first. She'd been so broken. But she was past that now and hoped she was a better person. Then when he broke… it was too much for the them to manage.

"You seem good," he said.

She nodded. "Thanks. You too. I'm glad we've had the chance to catch up again. It'll give us closure."

"Yeah, it feels right. I've wanted to apologise for a long time. I didn't think you'd want to see me."

"I was scared you'd blame me." She was being vulnerable with him, something she'd only learned to do recently. In the past, she would've put up a wall, shouted him down, pushed the blame onto his shoulders rather than facing it herself.

"I don't blame you. We were young," he replied, leaning forward on his board to paddle. "And what's done is done. We can't change the past."

"You're right," she said.

As he paddled away, she watched him go, then lay on her board to follow him. "We can't change the past. But we can learn to live with it," she whispered.

And maybe they'd even find friendship again. It was a lot to hope for, but these days she'd gotten better at allowing herself to hope. Still, there were things he didn't know. Things that might change the way he felt about her. Could they be friends if the truth was out in the open?

Chapter Four

Gwen Prince linked her hands behind her back to stroll around the sparkling swimming pool. She felt good for the first time in a long time. Her divorce was final. The inn she'd purchased with the money she got from the sale of her joint home with her husband was thriving. The renovation had cost more than she'd expected, but her contractor had done a fantastic job of bringing the old building back to life and giving it a personality that had resonated with guests. She was surprised every week by how many returning guests they had on their register—surprised and pleased.

And tonight was a celebration. Joanna Gilston's backyard had been transformed into a glamorous party venue for her grandson, Aaron's, engagement party. He was engaged to Joanna's former in-home carer, Emily. The two of them stood at the gift table, side by side, opening gifts. They were very sweet together.

Gwen stopped to watch them, a smile tugging at the corners of her mouth. She loved love. Even though her own marriage had ended in divorce after four children and almost four decades, she still believed in happily ever after. She enjoyed a good romance novel and watching romcoms on Netflix at the end of the day, and she'd delighted in observing from a distance as Aaron and Emily's real-life romance had played out in recent months. The two of them were very well suited to one another and, she hoped, much more likely to succeed in their marriage than she and Duncan had been. They were a few years older, and certainly more experienced in life than she and her ex were when they tied the knot.

Aaron had spent four years in the military, and Emily had gone through her share of hardships with a difficult family, what Gwen saw as fairly neglectful parents (although she hated to judge), and a sister who'd dealt with on-and-off bouts of cancer over the years with Emily as her only support. It seemed to her the engaged couple was going into marriage with eyes wide open and having retained their naturally kind and fun-loving dispositions even through the difficulties.

She noticed they were opening the gift she'd purchased them. She'd wrapped a set of stainless-steel saucepans in silver paper with a large silver bow attached. Emily read the card, then looked up at her with a smile. Gwen gave her a nod, then reached for a full glass of champagne on a nearby tray and took a sip as she watched them tear open the gift.

They both exclaimed over the large box, then Emily hurried over to thank Gwen. She embraced Gwen and kissed her on the cheek.

"Thank you. I love the gift."

Gwen laughed. "It's not much, but I think every home needs a good set of stainless-steel pots and pans. I hope you'll get a lot of use out of them."

"I know I will. I'm going to love cooking in those pots. It's the perfect gift."

Gwen rested a hand on Emily's arm and met her gaze with sincerity. "I'm barracking for the two of you. I know you'll have a wonderful marriage, and I wish you all the best."

"Thanks, Gwen. That means so much to me."

When Emily returned to stand by Aaron's side, Gwen continued into the house. She sipped her champagne, wondering where her best friends had gotten to. She found Joanna in the kitchen, slipping a tray of hor d'oeuvres out of the oven with a pair of oven mitts.

"There you are," Joanna said with a grin. "Could you help me get these onto a plate? Everyone has a big appetite tonight, it seems."

Gwen found a heavy white china tray in a nearby cupboard and began sliding the spring rolls and dumplings onto it with a spatula. "I can't believe you offered to cater this entire thing. It's much bigger than I expected. How many people are here?"

Joanna poured sauce into a ramekin to set beside the appetisers. "Um ... I think two hundred."

"That's a lot of people to fit into your house and backyard."

"Tell me about it," Joanna replied with a sigh. "Although, so far it seems to be working out okay."

"It's more than okay. You've done a fantastic job. I just think you probably should've asked for a little more help. You can't manage this all on your own."

"I've got you and Debbie," Joanna replied with a wry smile. "Right?"

"Of course you do," Gwen replied. "I'll get these out to the table and be right back to help with more. Speaking of which, where is Debbie?"

"She's filling glasses with champagne for the toasts."

"Perfect. I'll be back soon."

Gwen hurried out to the table with the tray of appetisers. As she stepped through the back sliding doorway, her foot caught on the lip of the door base and she tripped. She watched the tray, as though in slow motion, flying through the air. The ramekin was set free first—it disengaged from the tray and tipped sideways. Then the spring rolls were next, scattering in every direction. Followed by the dumplings, which dropped in clumps to the ground. Next, Gwen landed in the centre of the mess on her hands and knees just as the china tray shattered into pieces.

Everyone turned to stare at her. She felt the pain of it first in her neck. She must've twisted it somehow. It felt as though she couldn't turn her head without triggering a twinge. The group of people around the table fell silent. She felt very embarrassed. How had she missed that step? And all of Joanna's lovely appetisers were ruined. Just then, a pair of large, strong hands helped her to her feet.

"Thank you," she mumbled before looking up to find herself face-to-face with Mark Hunter, her contractor for the inn remodel.

His lined face was etched with concern. "Are you okay?"

She smoothed her dress with both hands. "I think so." She peered down at her legs. There didn't seem to be any blood. "Nothing broken."

He smiled. "I'm glad to hear that. Can I get you something? A drink?"

She shook her head. "No, I'm fine. Thanks. I have to clean this up and then get back into the kitchen to help Joanna. She's taken on a bit more than she can manage, I'm afraid. And I was supposed to be helping. Instead, I've caused a disaster."

Gwen bent to retrieve the appetisers, and Mark helped her. Then they found a dustpan and brush and swept up the pieces of the tray before someone stepped on them.

"Thank you for helping," she said, pushing a stray strand of hair behind her ear. "You didn't have to do that."

"I don't mind at all. It's nice to see you again." He offered her a warm smile, and it gave her a little jolt.

Was he flirting with her? No, she was crazy. Why would he do that? He was simply being nice because he was a kind man. She'd really enjoyed working with him. Every time she'd felt as though she might devolve into a panic attack over something going wrong at the inn, he'd talked her down and helped her to see the bigger picture. He'd been a rock through the entire process. But she'd always assumed he was married. Someone like him—tall, strong, handsome and nice—there was no way he was single. Anyway, it'd been so long since anyone flirted with her, she wasn't certain she'd even recognise it if it *did* happen.

"I'd better get back to the kitchen and break the bad news about the spring rolls to Joanna," Gwen said with a sigh. "Thanks again."

"No problem at all," he replied.

As she hurried into the house, she could've sworn he was still watching her, but she didn't dare turn around to find out.

Chapter Five

"I'll put that offer through, Mrs. Downtree, but I think I can safely say you've bought yourself a lovely beachside home. I'll call you back with the congratulations just as soon as it's confirmed with the seller."

Jemma hung up the phone with a grin of triumph on her face. Today was going well. She'd taken to real estate like a fish to water, and she still enjoyed closing a sale just as much today as she had five years ago when she'd made her first commission.

She called the seller to confirm, and as she'd expected, they accepted the offer. It was official. Now she only had to let the buyer know and file the paperwork. Dan would be happy. It'd been his dream to open a realty together, and for the first few years, it'd been touch and go on whether or not they'd manage to keep the business open. But in the last year, things had turned around. The market on Bribie Island had surged. They'd been well-positioned to take advantage of it. And after several years in the business, they'd finally established themselves as a brand that people trusted. The result had been a growing base of sales that promised good returns into the future. So far, they'd been paying off a lot of the debt they'd accumulated in setting up the business and running it over the leaner years, but soon they'd be able to start saving in earnest. And they might even be able to move out of their unit and buy themselves a little slice of real estate heaven in Sunshine.

"I sold another one!" she shouted as she leaned back in her rolling office chair to peer into the kitchenette, where Dan was making them a cup of tea each.

Dan tossed the tea bags into the bin with a laugh. "That's great news! You're on fire this month."

She called the buyer back to confirm and then got started on the paperwork. Dan set her cup of tea on the desk and then leaned against it to sip his, watching her work.

"Did you know that you always frown when you're concentrating?"

She shook her head, consciously making an effort not to frown. "So?"

"So, you'll get wrinkles."

Her eyes narrowed as she focused them on him. "I'll get wrinkles? That's what you're worried about?"

"You're too pretty to get wrinkles."

Sometimes she wondered what he was thinking, and then at times like this, she wished he would keep his thoughts to himself. "Thanks a lot."

He chuckled. "I'm just looking out for you, kid. This face is the moneymaker." He reached down to squeeze her cheeks.

She pulled her face free and glowered at him. "I'm not selling houses with my face. It's got nothing to do with how I look…"

"You're photogenic, and you look great on all our marketing materials. It definitely impacts sales. You're naïve if you don't realise that. Anyway, I'm trying to give you a compliment. Sometimes you're so difficult."

He shifted away from her desk and sat at his own near the window. He was sulking now. She rolled her eyes at his back.

They were trying so hard to have a baby, but maybe she should just accept that he was the only big baby she'd ever have. She let out a sigh.

That reminded her—she hadn't done a pregnancy test this month yet. Or last month, come to think of it. Another sigh. She reached into her desk drawer where there was a stack of tests still in their boxes. Her hand hovered over the stack. Did she want to do the test? It would just be another sock in the gut. She wouldn't be pregnant, just as she hadn't been for the previous countless tests she'd done. And she'd feel the exact same sinking feeling inside, as though it was never going to happen and she'd have to let go of her dream of becoming a mother. She wasn't ready to let go of it yet, but maybe it was time. They could have fulfilling lives together, just the two of them.

Dan let out an enormous burp, then laughed. "Did you hear that?"

Just the two of them? She groaned. "I could hardly miss it. What is with you today? Are you trying to be super annoying?"

He frowned. "Don't be a grouch."

When he acted like this, she wanted nothing more than to get away from him. She needed some alone time. She'd run the pregnancy test and then she'd go for a stroll, grab a coffee. She was tired, lagging. Maybe she was coming down with something. But the cup of tea just wasn't going to do it. A cappuccino was what she needed. Then she could finish the paperwork and perhaps she'd head home early—go to the beach and watch the sunset. There was something special about spending time close to the ocean. It always calmed her nerves and helped her feel better.

She carried a pregnancy test to the bathroom. Five minutes later, she stood at the sink, staring at the test with her mouth agape.

Positive.

She blinked. Pregnant again. Would it stick this time?

Maybe she could enjoy it. Not worry. Just live in the moment. A smile crept across her face, and joy bubbled in her gut. She was going to have a baby! With a rush of excitement, she ran out of the bathroom and back into the office, where she found her husband staring into the bottom of his empty tea mug.

"It wasn't enough," he said, turning to look at her. "I'm going to make another one. You want a second cup?" He rose to his feet, about to head for the kitchen, stopping when he saw the look on her face. "What?"

She raised the pregnancy test into the air between them, grinning widely.

Frowning, he stepped closer. "What's that? Oh..."

She laughed. "It's positive."

His eyebrows rose high. "You're pregnant?"

She nodded enthusiastically, waiting for the penny to drop.

He smiled and threw his arms around her. "That's amazing! We're having a baby. Wow!" But his words sounded a little hollow.

He was cautious. She got it. But she didn't want to live that way. Not any longer. She would embrace this pregnancy. She leaned into his chest. They would have this baby, and everything would be perfect. The tension between them would be gone, and they could go back to being head over heels in love again. The stress of getting pregnant had been hard on both of them and their relationship. But now, that was in the past. If she could only make it through the first trimester, they would be on their way to a blissful life as a family of three. All her dreams were coming true. Tears pricked at her eyes, and she jumped up and down, still in his embrace. Her head bumped his chin.

"Ouch!" he exclaimed, pushing away from her with a hand pressed to his chin.

"Sorry," she said. "I'm so excited, I can't help it. We're finally going to be a family."

He grimaced, rubbing his chin. "We're already a family, Smalls."

He called her Smalls sometimes. It was a nickname he'd given her when they were dating, and for some reason, it'd stuck. Probably because he was over six feet tall, and she was closer to five feet. She was petite, he was tall. It made sense, although she'd never much liked the name. It made her feel ... well, little.

"I know we're already a family. I mean, we're *having* a family. That's just what people call it when you have kids."

He sighed. "I'm happy about it, but the timing could've been better."

She frowned. "What do you mean?"

"We're getting the business going ... you're the face of the business. Things are ramping up, sales are growing, and we're paying off the loan. But what happens now? You'll take time off to have the baby, and we'll lose momentum."

"You'll still be here," she objected, feeling her joy slowly dissipate at his words.

"I'll still be here," he agreed. "But the clients want you. Don't ask me why, but they do. And now we're going to lose all of the hard work we've put into growing our market share." Another sigh. "But I suppose there's nothing we can do about that now."

She crossed her arms over her chest. He was ruining this moment. They'd been trying to get pregnant for so long. It was their dream—at least, she'd believed it was until now. Maybe it'd been *her* dream, and she'd simply believed he shared it with her. Maybe it was all in her head.

"It's simple—we'll put your face on all the new billboards.

We'll change direction and have you as the point of contact for clients going forward. I'll take over the marketing and admin you've been doing. We'll switch places. It'll be fine."

She couldn't believe he was worrying about real estate at a time like this. They were having a baby! They'd figure the rest out.

He rolled his eyes. "That will put us back to square one."

"I don't think so—we still have name recognition, and we share the same last name. Instead of Jemma Grant on the marketing materials, it will say Dan Grant. No big deal."

"No big deal? Only everything we've worked for…"

"None of that matters compared to building our family. This is what we've worked toward. We've done all of it for us —for our family, to have a life together. What's business without family?"

She didn't understand him. Maybe she never had. How could he fixate on business when all she could think about was the baby they were bringing into the world? For all she cared, the business could sink—the only reason it existed was to provide a roof over their heads and food for their child. Otherwise, it was meaningless to her in comparison to the prospect of becoming a mother.

He shook his head. "I can't believe you said that."

"And I can't believe this is what you want to talk about right now!" she snapped, her voice breaking on the words.

"Don't turn this around. You're the one being irrational and inconsiderate. You know how much the business means to me. Making it work is all I've thought of night and day for years."

"Maybe you should think about something else for a change then!" she shouted, then spun on her heel and ran out of the office.

As she marched down the street, dodging the foot traffic, she dashed tears from her eyes with the back of her hand. He was impossible to please. Everything she did was wrong. Everything she said offended him. She couldn't win. This should've been a loving celebration between husband and wife, and now all she could think about was getting away from him to spend some time on her own. How could they be parents when they could barely get through one conversation without arguing? And when did her husband become so obsessed with money and success that he couldn't think about anything else?

He put so much pressure on her to succeed in real estate. But real estate wasn't her dream. Having a family was what she longed for. And he didn't seem to care as much about their family as he did making money. The thought broke her heart and sent tears streaming down her cheeks.

Chapter Six

The cloud of hairspray hung in the air, making Maree cough. She ducked out of the bathroom and gasped in a lungful of fresh air. That was better. After she flicked on the bathroom fan, it didn't take long for the hairspray to drift toward the ceiling, and she stepped back into the bathroom to survey her reflection. She'd gone a bit over the top with the spray, but her freshly curled hair looked decent. Not as good as the hairdresser did when Maree got her blonde highlights refreshed, but pretty good. And her makeup wasn't half bad for someone who rarely wore the stuff.

She turned her head to check that she hadn't inadvertently missed anything obvious, then slipped on a buttoned silk shirt over her ripped jeans. Tonight was Emily's hens party, and she was looking forward to it.

She and Emily Miller had been friends since high school. They weren't particularly close, but then, she wasn't sure Emily was very close with many people. She had a tight-knit group of older women she seemed to spend most of her time with, plus her sister, Wanda. But when she wanted to go out with friends, she usually called Maree and Jemma. And tonight, they were going out as a trio to celebrate Emily's upcoming wedding to Aaron Gilston. Sam was staying with a babysitter Maree used on the odd occasion that both she and Jemma were busy. He loved it, and it gave Maree a much-needed break, although she couldn't afford to do it often.

Maree smiled at her reflection as she remembered Aaron from high school, her dimples deepening. He'd been the handsome bad boy. The jock who'd excelled at everything. And Emily had been madly in love with him, even though she rarely said a word about it. She'd been quiet and shy throughout their school years, but everyone knew she was smitten with Aaron. And she'd been heartbroken when he left to join the Army after graduation.

It was truly the most romantic love story Maree had ever watched play out in real life—the two of them finding each other all these years later. It made her feel warm and gooey inside. But then she remembered how her own happily ever after had worked out, and the warmth quickly faded, along with her smile.

Oh, well. Some things just weren't meant to be, and apparently her marital happiness was one of those things. But she'd moved on. She'd rebuilt her life on her own and she believed she'd find happiness again someday—even if she had to be alone, she'd find a way to thrive.

Meanwhile, she had a celebration to attend, and even though she was tired after a long day working at the inn, she was happy for Emily. She had never seen her friend so content.

She found Jemma waiting for her in the kitchen, sipping a cup of tea. "Ready to go?"

Maree smiled. "I really want to crawl into bed and watch a movie on Netflix."

Jemma laughed. "I know exactly what you mean. I feel like I'm about to collapse. I'm hoping this tea will help."

"But we're going to put on a big smile and paint the town

red!" Maree trilled in the most enthusiastic voice she could muster. She followed it up with an enormous yawn. This wouldn't do. "I'm going to buy a coffee on the way there."

The party was starting at the Black Cat Café. From there, they planned on a round of mini putt-putt with cocktails. Maree was determined to make it as enjoyable as possible even if her life as a single working and studying mother left her constantly exhausted. She wanted Emily to have the best night. And if she and Jemma weren't full of energy, they could pretend. In their younger years, they'd gone out dancing until the wee hours. Surely they could muster up the energy for a game of mini golf.

As she collected her cappuccino from a coffee cart on the beach side of the street, she said, "We're really not that old. We should be ready to party at a moment's notice. Right?"

"I'm ready to party. So ready." Jemma's yawn almost split her face in two.

"We're hopeless," Maree said with a laugh. "You want a coffee too? It might help."

Jemma shook her head. "No thanks. I'm avoiding caffeine."

Maree sipped her coffee as they walked along the beach path towards the café.

"I saw Jack the other day," she said suddenly.

Jemma gaped. "What? Why didn't you tell me? Where was he?"

"He was eating at the inn with his family. He's moved back to Sunshine."

"Wow! How do you feel about that?"

Maree inhaled a slow breath. She didn't know how she felt. She hadn't given herself time to consider the implications. She was simply trying to get through each day. Learning her new role at the inn and surviving was taking all of her energy.

"It's fine," she said with a forced smile. "I've moved on. I don't care what he does. His family lives here, and Jack has every right to live here as well. After all, they're almost an institution on the island. It makes sense he'd want to come back, whereas I'm the blow-in. I've spent my life here, but I'm first generation in Sunshine. They've been here forever."

Jemma's eyes narrowed. "I don't think that's really relevant. And you're not a blow-in. You have as much right to call Sunshine home as anyone does. And besides, you didn't really answer my question."

"You noticed that, huh?" She chuckled. "I can't ever get anything past you."

"Are you okay seeing him again?"

"I guess so. Although it's weird."

"Very weird," Jemma agreed. "I wonder if he's coming to this thing."

"What do you mean?"

"They're doing a combined bucks and hens night. And Jack was always close with Aaron. They were tight in high school, and from what I understand, they've always kept in touch. You didn't know?"

Nerves jangled in Maree's gut. It made sense that Aaron would've invited Jack, but she'd somehow missed the announcement that there'd be men at the event. "No, I didn't realise."

* * *

Jemma was right. Aaron had invited Jack. Maree saw him as soon as they walked into the café. He stood against the far wall, with a drink, chatting with Emily and Aaron, who looked adorable beside him, hand in hand.

Maree swallowed hard, willing the butterflies in her stomach to calm down. So, Jack was here. It didn't matter to her. Going surfing together had made things less awkward between them. But she still wasn't used to seeing him around. She'd have to accept that this was her new normal. That or move. But the problem with that was, she didn't have any money. Moving wasn't an option, at least not in the near future. She couldn't afford to give up her job, and didn't have enough saved for a security deposit somewhere new.

Since she was currently rooming with Jemma and Dan, their cheap rent was the only thing keeping her head above water. The irony of a future financial planner living paycheck to paycheck wasn't lost on her. But her never-ending fight to make ends meet was what first attracted her to the field, and she couldn't wait until she was finally qualified to become a professional planner. Maybe then she could leave Sunshine and get away from her ex-husband and his family for good. She needed a fresh start. But she wasn't going to get that anytime soon.

"Hi, Maree," Jack said, turning to greet her. His eyes sparkled, and she felt her knees go weak, the way they always had around Jack Houston. "I thought I might see you here."

She offered him a wan smile. "I had no idea you'd be here."

He laughed. "Can I get you a drink?"

"I'm fine, thanks. Hi, Emily, Aaron. Congratulations on the upcoming wedding." She turned her attention to the happy couple, anxious to get out of the tractor beam of Jack's gaze.

Emily grabbed her by the arm and pulled her away. "I'm sorry—I forgot to tell you that Aaron invited Jack. 'Forgot' is the wrong word. What I meant to say is that my fiancé is a doofus who didn't mention it until this morning. And then was absolutely dumbfounded as to why I might have an issue with that."

"It's fine," Maree replied. She had a feeling she was going to be using those words a lot. Fine. Everything was fine. She was fine. He was fine. The whole situation was fine.

"I'm sorry, I should've warned you. Are you okay?"

"I'm fine." There it was again.

Emily studied her face. "Well, if you're sure."

"I am sure. Aaron and Jack are friends. It makes sense he'd want to invite him. And anyway, Jack and I have been divorced for five years. It's time we put the past behind us and moved on. We loved each other once; it didn't work out. These things happen."

Emily tipped her head to one side. "You're very Zen about this. It's freaking me out."

Maree laughed. "Don't worry so much. I promise, I'll let you know if I have an issue. Or I'll go home. One or the other. But right now, I want to celebrate you. This is your night. And I'm determined that you're going to have a good time."

Chapter Seven

Maree loved Christmas. Christmas was her favourite time of year. At least, it had been up until the divorce. She and Jack had made it special, just the two of them. She hadn't been close with her family growing up, so when the two of them got married, she readily embraced his family, and they'd welcomed her in with open arms. She'd adopted their Christmas traditions and happily carried her bowl of stuffing over to his parents' mansion on Christmas Day. She'd been completely and utterly happy for those few brief Christmases.

Now, she wasn't sure how she felt about the holiday. Since their breakup, she'd travelled to see her mother. But spending the holiday with a stepfamily who did nothing more than drink and get into arguments about politics that often devolved into all-out shouting matches wasn't exactly her idea of a good time. She often spent much of the day in the guest bedroom with the door shut, watching Hallmark movies on her iPhone. If she could escape reality and pretend she was in an idyllic setting where family mattered, and the heat could be replaced by a snow-covered wonderland, she would do it.

But this Christmas, she wasn't sure she could muster the

energy to face all of that again. Maybe they'd have Christmas on their own — just her and Sam.

"Penny for your thoughts," Jemma said, as she slid into a chair beside Maree.

She had purposely chosen the seat by the café's window so she could have a little space from the rest of the group, but she was grateful to have Jemma by her side.

"I'm thinking about Christmas. Have you and Dan decided what you'll do this year?"

Jemma nodded. "We're staying home. I'm not feeling ... up to doing too much. So, we're going to have a quiet one. And besides, our families are both travelling this year to visit relatives."

"Do you mind if we join you? It's okay if you'd rather not..."

She grinned and reached for Maree's hand, squeezing it. "I would love you to be there. That will make the holiday so much better."

A lump formed in Maree's throat. She was so grateful for Jemma and Emily. She wasn't sure how she would've managed the past few years without the two of them.

As they ate dinner, Maree began to relax. Jack sat at the other end of the table, and she spent most of the meal chatting with Jemma and Emily. While Jack was absorbed in a discussion with Aaron and Tristan, Emily's brother and one of Aaron's closest friends. Every now and then, Maree would glance at Jack and her heart would skip a beat. He'd always been so handsome.

"Golf time!" Emily said, standing to her feet. "Let's walk to the mini putt-putt course. It's so lovely at this time of night and it isn't very far."

Chattering and laughing, they all traipsed out of the café and along the beach. Maree kicked off her sandals and held them in one hand. The sand was cool on her feet and a little damp from the evening air and the earlier high tide. Nearby, a gull cried, then fell silent. The full moon left a silver trail across the surface of the glistening ocean. It was breathtaking, and Maree fell under its spell as she strolled in silence beside the rowdy group.

"You always loved walking on the beach," Jack said, falling into step behind her. He also held his sandals in one hand, his toes pushing deep into the sand with each step.

She glanced up at him, her nerves gone. There was no need for them to be tense with one another. What'd happened between them was long since buried in the past. They'd been best friends before they fell in love, and she still held a lot of affection for him now.

"It's so peaceful," she said. "You can forget about the rest of the world."

She wished she could see his grey eyes better. She could always tell what he was thinking from his eyes. But it was dark, and all she could see was the outline of his face.

"How are you? Really?" His voice was soft, intense.

She couldn't help smiling. "I'm fine. Really, I am."

"And you don't mind that I'm back in town?"

"I'm glad," she said, and it felt true for the first time. "It's nice to see you again. It's been a long time."

"Five years," he agreed. "Far too long."

"It's been five years, but tonight it feels like we're back in high school. All the old crowd together again."

He laughed. "You're right, it does. It's a bit surreal."

"Let's race to the jetty!" Aaron cried suddenly.

"Piggyback!" Emily added before leaping onto Aaron's back, almost sending him tumbling to the sand.

Laughing, he began to run with her perched, her legs wrapped around his hips. Then Jemma climbed onto Dan's back, and the four of them raced down the beach together.

Maree stopped to watch them, her heart light.

Jack whistled. "They're crazy."

She turned to face him. The moonlight shone on his face, making him seem ethereal for a moment. And she flashed back to a time when they'd snuck out of their houses to meet on the beach in the middle of the night once, when they were sixteen years old. Their parents had tried to keep them apart, saying their relationship was too intense. But they'd been determined to be together even if it meant they had to meet in secret.

They'd found a little nook near the jetty, hidden away from the footpath by a cluster of black rocks. Huddled in that tiny, secret space, they'd talked and kissed for hours. The memory of his lips on hers made her bite her lower lip. His touch was probably the thing she missed most.

"What are you thinking about?" he asked, one eyebrow quirked.

She exhaled, not realising she'd been holding her breath until that second. "I was thinking about that time we met here on the beach in the middle of the night. They were so angry when they found our beds empty. Do you remember that?"

"I remember a lot of kissing," he replied, echoing her thoughts.

A tingle ran up her arms and down her back at the memory. Those kisses were everything to her at the time. She couldn't get enough of his lips. Couldn't imagine a safer place than in his arms. Where did they go wrong?

"We definitely clocked some hours with our lips locked," she agreed with a laugh.

"No one has ever kissed as much as we did, before or since," he agreed.

She grinned. "We were good at it."

"Why did we ever stop?" he asked, staring at her, his eyes like deep pools and his smile fading.

"I do wonder that myself sometimes," she replied. What did they fight about? She couldn't recall. Her mind was a fog of desire. All she could think about were his lips. This was a disaster. When she was around him, all rationality fled.

"Do you remember our last kiss?" he asked.

This conversation was fast becoming dangerous. She should change the subject. She glanced at the end of the beach, where their four friends had all fallen in a laughing pile on the sand.

"I can't recall," she said. "Whenever it was, I guess we didn't realise it would be the last, so we didn't commit it to memory."

He stepped toward her, his hand brushing against the back of hers. He was too close. She couldn't think clearly. Her head felt light. Every nerve end was on fire.

"We didn't know it would be the last, so we didn't enjoy it as much as we should've. Your kisses ... Phew." He sighed. "I've missed them."

"Jack..." she objected.

"I know, I'm not going there. Trust me, I realise you've moved on, and we have no future together. I just thought, it might be a good idea to get that closure now."

She frowned. "What do you mean?"

"We could have our last kiss. That way, we'd both know it's the last one. We'd enjoy it, commit it to memory, and then put it behind us. We can leave the past where it belongs and move forward."

His words made sense to her in a twisted kind of way, but it was a terrible idea. It would reawaken old feelings. Wouldn't it? "That sounds like playing with fire."

He took another step closer so that his breath tickled her hair. "You're not going to fall back in love with me again, are you?"

She huffed. "No, of course not."

"And I'm not going to fall back in love with you."

"Okay, good to know..."

"So, what's the issue? I want closure, I'm sure you do too. So, let's give each other that closure. A sort of goodbye kiss, if you will."

"A goodbye kiss?"

He nodded and reached for her hand. As he entwined his fingers through hers, every cell in her body screamed out for more. But her mind fought against the impulse. This was wrong. It'd taken her so long to get over him, to rebuild her life after he left. She couldn't go back there again. But one kiss wouldn't mean anything, and maybe he was right. It would be nice to experience that connection with him one last time.

"I can't remember what it was like to kiss you..." she began.

And then his hands moved up to cup her cheeks as he pressed his lips to hers. His thumbs stroked her face as his lips moved against hers. Her lips parted slightly, and she felt his tongue caress them. Fireworks erupted in her belly and sent shooting pleasure throughout her. Her knees went weak, and she sank against his firm body, letting her hands wind around his neck. Her fingers combed through his hair as she grasped at it, pulling him down to deepen their kiss. He groaned against her mouth, making her wild inside.

Then he pulled away from her. Stepped back once, twice. He rubbed his fingers across his lips, breathing heavily.

"See? Closure," he said.

She nodded mutely, then watched as he jogged down the beach to join their friends. She sank into the sand, her legs unable to hold her up any longer. Closure? Is that what that was? If it was an ending to something, she couldn't imagine what. All she felt now was an intense desire to run down that beach and finish what they'd just started. But she couldn't. He was her ex-husband. And reigniting that particular fire would be a huge mistake.

Chapter Eight

Gwen pushed the last bite of Vegemite on toast into her mouth and chewed as she walked from the kitchen to her bedroom. She was running late for work. Things at the inn were so busy these days that she never slowed down. She was running to work or running at work or running home from work. Running, running, running. She'd lost ten kilograms and was fitter than she'd been in years. She liked the way she looked in the mirror and was able to fit into clothes she'd never have dreamed of wearing before her divorce.

She swallowed and quickly brushed her teeth, then turned one way and the other, surveying her reflection in the mirror. Her shoulder-length grey hair had a natural wave, and her blue eyes sparkled, even if there were smudges beneath them that she'd had to cover with concealer. She was tired. What she really needed was a rest. Some time away from work and grandchildren. Time to herself to relax. Maybe she should book a holiday somewhere. Nothing big, just a little bit of time off.

Her phone rang, and she grimaced. She didn't have time to talk to anyone. But what if it was important?

"Hello?"

"Hi, Gwen. It's Mark. How are you? I hope you're not injured from your fall."

She was glad to hear his voice. It calmed her nerves immediately. She hurried into the closet to grab her purse.

"Mark, how lovely. I'm just on my way to work. But I'll walk and talk at the same time. And thank you for asking, I'm well. I have two little bruises on my knees, but I'm sure they'll fade in no time. My neck is sore as well, but nothing that a heat pack can't help."

"Glad to hear it," he replied. "Although you should probably see a physiotherapist in case."

"You're right, of course. I'll make an appointment as soon as I get to work."

"Busy?" he asked.

She laughed. "Beyond busy. But I suppose that's a good thing, so I can't complain."

"You wouldn't want to have nothing to do."

"No, you're right. The inn has been more successful so far than I could've dreamed, although I'm acutely aware that could change at any time. The tourism industry is famously fickle."

"Well, I think you're onto a winner. I love the place. I ate there last week with my sister and her family."

"That's nice. I'm surprised I didn't see you."

"I spotted you rushing past but didn't want to bother you," he said.

She climbed into her car and turned on the ignition, letting the phone call switch to Bluetooth as she pulled out of the garage. "You would never be a bother. Please say hello next time."

"Okay, I'll do that."

She waited, and silence filled the car. Surely he'd called for a reason. She would give him time to explain.

"What are you up to today?"

She turned onto the main road, checking over her shoulder for oncoming traffic. "I'm going to be at the inn all morning and then I've got a function at the Rotary Club. They're fundraising for the Surf Life Savers, and I promised Debbie I'd be there."

"Oh, okay."

"Why do you ask?"

He cleared his throat. "I'm going down to the Riding for the Disabled Centre, and I thought you might like to come with me. You could ride one of their horses, and I could show you around. It's a great place. And the horses are very quiet."

Her eyes widened. Was this a date? She couldn't tell. But it sounded like fun, and she didn't really want to go to the fundraiser. "I could cancel on Debbie."

"Are you sure? I don't want to cause any trouble."

"You'd be doing me a favour. Horse riding sounds a lot more appealing to me right now. I need to have some downtime and do something enjoyable. My life has gotten far too pressured lately."

"That's great. I'll pick you up at the inn at two o'clock."

"Perfect."

* * *

The McLintock Stables were on the mainland, set beside a large brown river that wound along the coastline. It was picture perfect, with a long green field surrounded by a white picket fence. Horses grazed peacefully beside a row of stables.

"I love this place. I've driven by it so many times, but I've never stopped here. Do you volunteer often?" Gwen asked.

Mark smiled. "I come once a fortnight. It brings me a lot of joy to help the disabled children ride the horses. I'm not much of a horse rider myself, but I can lead a horse. And I've gotten pretty good at grooming them, understanding their body language, and so on."

She couldn't help being impressed by him. This big, burly construction manager who liked to help disabled children to ride horses. It was a very attractive quality—she couldn't deny it.

They climbed out of Mark's truck, and he went into a small timber office, leaving Gwen to wander around. She walked over to a yard and stood with one foot on the lower railing as she watched a foal feed from its mother. It was so sweet. This was exactly what she'd needed.

Mark soon returned with another woman. The woman smiled warmly and held out a hand. "Hi, I'm Heidi. You must be Gwen. Welcome to the McLintock Stables."

Gwen shook her hand. "Thank you so much. This place is wonderful."

"Thank you," Heidi said, her gaze taking in the entire scene with pride. "We like it. Mark tells me you've come to help out today. Is that right?"

"I'd love to help if I can. Although I'm not very experienced with horses or riding."

"But you're very experienced with children, from what I understand."

Gwen laughed. "That's true, if you count four kids and ten grandkids."

"That definitely counts," Heidi replied. "Don't worry about understanding horses. You can help Mark with his today. I'm sure he'll give you all the instruction you'll need."

"I'm looking forward to it," Gwen replied.

Mark took her to the stables, where he found a halter and lead. He carried them into the field, and they caught one of the horses—a chestnut mare called Molly. She was easy to catch, and she quickly searched his hand for a treat with her soft nose. He gave her a piece of carrot that she munched happily while he slipped the halter over her head. Then he gave the lead to Gwen, and she led the mare back to the stable and hitched her to a post.

"We'll saddle her now. The kids will be here soon."

He showed her how to put a rug on the horse's back, followed by the saddle, then how to tighten the girth. There were other volunteers there as well, catching and saddling the horses. Mark caught and saddled another one, this time a large bay gelding. While Gwen stood and tickled Molly's nose, a small white bus pulled into the long gravel driveway.

Kids soon piled out of the bus, laughing and chattering loudly. They all had different levels of disability. Some wouldn't ride but would interact with the horses and watch, while others were dressed and ready to climb onto the animals' backs.

Mark let Gwen lead Molly around while he led the gelding behind her. He kept an eye on her, but she didn't have any issues. The mare was sweet-tempered and quiet. She didn't give Gwen any trouble. Each of the children had a marvellous time riding. She could see the joy on their faces, and it made her heart swell with happiness.

Chapter Nine

Morning sickness was the worst. Jemma had visited her GP and discovered that she was now twelve weeks pregnant. She'd felt nauseated all day long and the only thing that helped was to eat, so she'd been snacking all day as well. If she kept this up, she'd gain twenty kilograms by the end of the pregnancy. Surely it couldn't stay this bad for the duration.

The good news was, she was through the first trimester, and she hadn't even realised she was pregnant. She'd simply thought her hormones were a little out of kilter, which wasn't unusual for her. She was through the danger zone. Now she really could celebrate them having a baby.

She leaned over the toilet bowl, waiting for the wave of nausea to pass. It did, but slowly. She stood and smoothed down her skirt. Her reflection in the mirror showed that her face was pale and her eyes red. She fixed her hair and studied the way her skirt fit snug over her flat stomach—this suit wouldn't work in a few weeks' time. Most of her wardrobe would be too tight and too small for her. She'd have to buy all new clothes. That thought would've excited her not so long ago, but now, with everything Dan had said, she wasn't sure what to think.

They'd been getting along well since their fight. They'd had fun at the bachelor/bachelorette parties for Aaron and Emily. It'd been like old times with their oldest friends, but his words lingered in her thoughts.

In the kitchen, she poured herself a coffee, then thought again and poured it out in the sink. She kept forgetting that she couldn't drink caffeine. But what could she have that would wake her up and wouldn't make her sick? She sighed and reached for an herbal tea bag. It would have to do.

It was Saturday, and she was supposed to be at the office, but she was exhausted. All she wanted to do was get back into her PJs and climb into bed. She had two open houses that day, but maybe Dan could do them for her. He'd have to take on more of that work over the coming months anyway. And it wouldn't look good for her to be constantly running off to the bathroom. She sent Dan a text message and waited for his response.

He sent a terse reply saying he would do the open houses, but he was really busy. She ignored the snark and thanked him, then padded down the hallway with her cup of tea. She peeled off her business suit and pulled the soft shirt of her PJs over her head, climbed into bed. With the tea mug on her bedside table, she searched her phone for some soothing music and hit play. Then she snuggled down under the covers.

Maree had already gone to work at the inn and taken Sam to daycare, so she was alone in the apartment. It felt so nice not to have to go anywhere or to take care of anyone. She could simply exist and relax. She hadn't done that in a long time. Maybe she should watch a movie. How luxurious. From what everyone told her, she wouldn't have much time for that after the baby came, and she should take advantage of this opportunity.

There was a small TV screen on their bedroom wall. She flicked through the options and selected a Jane Austen romance before plumping the pillows behind her head. As the opening credits filled the screen, she couldn't help wondering how Dan would cope with the changes to their lifestyle that were ahead for them. And what about Maree? She was living in the room that would become the nursery. Either Jemma and Dan should move or Maree would have to leave.

They'd been saving a deposit for a house for a while now, although with the loan repayments to make, they hadn't managed to save much. Which meant that since she'd shown Dan the pregnancy test, he'd taken to working night and day. She'd hardly seen him apart from the previous evening with their friends. She understood—he was stressed about providing for their burgeoning family, but she wished she could spend a little time with him so they could celebrate together and enjoy this special time. Even if he was home in the evenings, she was in bed so early that it wouldn't make much difference. Still, the thought that he was there would be a comfort to her.

She found it difficult to focus on the movie. All she could think about was the way Dan had reacted to her pregnancy. She didn't want to work full time once the baby was born. She didn't want to be the kind of mother who was always gone or rushing from one thing to the next. She'd had those kinds of parents and always felt as though she was their last priority. She couldn't do that to her child, especially given how much she'd hoped and prayed for this baby.

Maybe Dan would come around. But she couldn't help wondering sometimes who he was now —he'd changed, wasn't the same carefree, happy and easygoing boy she'd met in high school. And it was hard not to think about whether she'd made the right choice in marrying him. She loved him, and she was certain he loved her. But was love enough?

Chapter Ten

It was a very hot morning. Sweat beaded on Maree's forehead and trickled down the sides of her face as she turned the key in the ignition again. And again, nothing happened. In the back seat, Sam was whining.

"I'm hot. I don't like yoghurt. I don't want it."

She'd given him a squeezy yogurt for breakfast because they were running late for daycare, and subsequently for work, and she didn't have time to make his porridge today. He wasn't a big fan of changes to their routine.

With the back of her hand, she dashed away the sweat from her forehead and tried again. "Come on..." she whispered.

Her car had a tendency to be temperamental, but it usually started at some point. She just had to jiggle the key the right way in the ignition, and it would putter to life. But not today. The engine didn't even issue a sound. Not a complaint or an attempt, or anything remotely like a putter.

"I'm hungry. I don't want yoghurt." Sam's complaints were growing in volume. He couldn't stay in the car—it was far too hot. She wound down the windows and a slight breeze drifted through, cooling them both.

"I just have to call the tow truck. I'm not sure what's wrong with the car, buddy. But I think it's probably the battery."

She didn't know much about vehicles. But she topped up the oil every week, since her car leaked like a stuck pig. And she knew it was probably about time for a new battery, although she wasn't sure what to do about it. She needed to get to daycare to drop off Sam and to work for her shift at the inn. But she couldn't do either unless she called a taxi, and that would cost more than she had in her bank account, since it wasn't payday until tomorrow.

It was then she realised she'd left her phone in the apartment. She glanced up at the second floor. She couldn't see the apartment door but could spot the open windows of her neighbour's apartment. Mr Sanchez had lived there as long as she'd been a resident. He was a friendly older man who always offered to help. Perhaps she could call out to him to give her a hand. The thought of wrangling Sam back up the stairs again so she could find her phone was more than she could bear at the moment. It'd been hard enough to get him down the stairs and into the car in the first place.

She climbed out and cupped her hands around her mouth. "Mr Sanchez!" There was no response, so she repeated the call a couple more times, growing increasingly embarrassed.

What was she thinking? She shouldn't be shouting her neighbour's name. She'd have to go back upstairs and call in sick. But then what would happen for Christmas? She could barely afford to buy Sam the few small things she'd planned for the holiday with the wages she had working part time at the inn. If she missed a shift, that paycheck would drop dramatically, and she wouldn't be able to buy him any gifts.

The thought made her heart squeeze. She glanced back at his sweet little face, growing redder by the moment, and she wished she could change their lives to make it better for him. But she was doing that as fast as she could, studying to give herself the qualifications for a better career. It would take time, but she was determined to work for their future.

Just then, a head appeared at the window, framed by the thin white curtains that flapped in the breeze behind him. Her heart jumped into her throat. It was Jack. What was he doing in Mr Sanchez's apartment? He was shirtless, his muscular torso glistening with sweat—no doubt he'd just returned from his routine morning run. She remembered it all very vividly. He was a creature of habit, and he never missed his early workout.

She tented a hand over her eyes, squinting against the bright sun. The figure disappeared. Perhaps she was imagining things. She had Jack on the brain after their kiss. She hadn't been able to stop thinking about him, constantly worrying over the next time they might run into one another. What would she say? How should she act? What did closure really mean?

Maree was in the middle of handing Sam a bottle of cold water out of his daycare bag when she heard a deep voice behind her. She straightened and spun around to find herself face-to-face with Jack.

"Are you okay?" he asked, concern etching his handsome features. He was still shirtless, wearing only a pair of athletic shorts and joggers. His torso glistened under the harsh glare of the sun.

"Um ... hi, Jack. What are you doing here?" She glanced nervously back at Mr Sanchez's apartment. "Do you know Mr. Sanchez?" It was pretty early in the morning to be visiting a friend, if that's what he was.

Jack grinned. "I'm your new neighbour. Mr Sanchez moved out a few weeks ago, and I took up his lease."

She hadn't seen her neighbour in a while, so that made sense. But Jack had moved in? "How? ... What? ... Why?" she stammered, unable to form a sentence. Her mind was in a whirl. This couldn't be happening. Her ex-husband had moved into the apartment across the corridor from her own. She never could have seen this coming.

He laughed. "Breathe, Maree. I'm not going to bother you, I promise. Dan knew I was looking for a place, and he told me this one was open. I love the location—it's so close to the beach. And the price was right."

"You're not living with your family?"

"I'm a bit too old for that. So, what did you want Mr Sanchez for?"

She blinked. "Oh, yeah. My car won't start."

Jack scanned the vehicle. "You still have this old thing? I'm not surprised it won't start. It wasn't great five years ago. I wanted to get you something newer—you should've let me."

"I didn't think I needed it. And now I can't afford anything more." She bit down on her tongue. The last thing she wanted was for her ex-husband to know how much she was struggling. Shame washed over her. She wanted him to believe she'd thrived ever since he walked out.

"I'll pull mine up and give you a jump," he said. "It's right over here."

He pointed at a brand-new truck with a flash red paint job. It looked as though it'd cost a fortune. But that wasn't surprising. Jack's family was wealthy, and he worked as a physiotherapist in the city, had his own practice. He likely had a pretty fat bank account. Not that she cared. It didn't make any difference to her life how much money he had. And money had never been something she was particularly interested in—

until she became a mother and realised how difficult it was to raise a child without any.

"It's really not necessary. I was about to call RACQ, but I left my phone up in the apartment. That's why I was calling out. I hoped Mr Sanchez might call them for me."

"Do you have a membership with them?" he asked.

She grimaced. "I meant to get one, but I didn't get around to it."

He smiled. "It's fine. I'm sure we can jump it. But if we can't, then I'll drive you to get a new battery."

With a sigh, she agreed. There was no way around it. Even if she went upstairs now to get her phone, she couldn't afford the membership with the motor club. And she didn't have enough money in her account to buy a new battery, either. She wasn't sure what she'd do.

"I need to run upstairs," she said. "Can you watch Sam?"

He blinked. "Sam? Who's Sam?"

She stepped away from the car and waved at the back seat. Sam looked at him through the window. His big brown eyes were bored, and his face was red from the heat. "Sam is my son."

Jack smiled at him. "Hey, Sam. I'm Jack. Your mum has to run up to the apartment for a minute. Is that okay with you?"

"I'm thirsty."

"You've got your water bottle," Maree replied, leaning through the car window to ruffle Sam's hair. "And if you get too hot, you can stand out here with Jack. I won't be long."

"Okay," Sam said, letting his head rest on the back of the seat.

She took a step away from the car before Jack spoke. "How old is Sam?"

Maree's heart skipped a beat. She spun to face him, plastering a smile across her lips. "He's four, almost five."

"Oh?" His eyes narrowed as he processed that information. Then he glanced back at Sam. "He's a handsome kid."

She nodded. "Uh-huh. He's the best. I won't be long."

"Who's the father?"

Her stomach twisted into a knot. "My fiancé." Why did she say that? She couldn't think straight when he was standing next to her. Jack made her crazy. He'd always had that effect on her, and now she'd outright lied to him. He was living next door. It wouldn't take him long to figure out that she didn't have a fiancé. Or a boyfriend, for that matter. She hadn't dated since the divorce. She'd been too busy taking care of Sam.

His eyes widened in surprise. "You're getting married?"

The knot in her stomach grew. "That's right."

"You shouldn't marry him," he replied, his eyes growing dark. "You're my wife."

"I *was* your wife," she corrected him. "And then you walked away from us and didn't look back. It was your choice, Jack. Not mine. Don't make me feel bad for it."

His nostrils flared. "You know why I did that. I was grieving. Young. Stupid. I made a mistake. It was the biggest regret of my life."

Her heart squeezed at his words. He'd never said that before. She'd always assumed he'd been happy with his choice. That he'd sailed off into the sunset and built a life for himself full of joy and love, a life that didn't include her.

"You regret it?" she asked.

He looked stricken. "More than anything. I wouldn't have done it if it hadn't been for the accident. I thought you realised that."

She shook her head. "I didn't know anything. I was young too, you forget. My insecurities got the better of me. I thought you hated me."

He grunted. "Never."

"Look, I've got to hurry. It's too hot out here for Sam to stay in the car. I need my phone and credit card."

As she ran up the stairs to the apartment, her heart raced. Leaving her had been a mistake? She didn't understand why he would say that. He hadn't been back to see her in five years, hadn't picked up the phone to call her. Surely he would've done either of those things, or both, if he really regretted his decision. She hadn't gone anywhere. She was still in the same place he'd left her. Still had the same mobile number. He could've contacted her anytime he wanted to, but he didn't. She wasn't sure she could ever forgive him for that, no matter how good he looked without a shirt, or how contrite he seemed.

Chapter Eleven

Jack had brought his own truck over to jump-start her vehicle, and when Maree got back downstairs with her phone and credit card, she was grateful to see he'd placed Sam in the back seat of his truck with the air-conditioning running. He'd also given Sam his phone, and the little boy was laughing hysterically over a cartoon while they worked on her car.

"Thanks," she said, nodding her head in Sam's direction as he burst out into another gale of laughter inside the truck.

He leaned over the car engine and twisted the connections. "No worries. He seems like a good kid."

"He is. The best," she replied. "I only wish..."

He straightened and wiped his hands on his shorts. "Wish what?"

"Oh, nothing."

"You can tell me. It's okay."

She inhaled a sharp breath. "I wish I could get him something nice for Christmas. But I'm getting a car battery instead. Yay!" She pumped her fists in the air with a groan.

He smiled, his eyes full of sympathy. "I'm sure he understands."

"He's four. He doesn't have much insight into the financial demands of single motherhood."

"His dad doesn't help at all?" Jack asked.

She realised with a jolt that she'd just poked a hole in her own story. What kind of father, and fiancé, wouldn't help her buy their son a Christmas gift? "Oh . . . um, he's a struggling artist, so he doesn't have much money himself." Great save. She wanted to smack herself in the forehead.

He didn't say a word as he simply climbed into his vehicle to start the engine. She did the same in hers, and there was no response.

"I think it's dead," she said, getting back out of the car.

He nodded. "Come on—get in. I'll drive you to wherever you're going. You can deal with this later."

She didn't have the energy to argue with him, so she grabbed her bag and Sam's backpack from the car and locked it up. As she climbed into the passenger seat of the truck, the nice, cool air washed over her, and she leaned against the headrest with a sigh of pleasure.

"Better?" he asked, adjusting the fans so they angled toward her face.

"Much," she replied.

"Where are we headed?"

"Daycare first, and then the inn."

They chatted about nothing much on the way. Sam was completely unbothered by the change of situation other than constantly praising the truck and asking if they could get one for Christmas as she walked him to his classroom. Then Jack drove her to the inn.

"Thanks for doing this. I really appreciate it."

He nodded.

"You didn't have to, though."

"I know that," he said. "I wanted to."

"Well, thanks." She'd simply have to catch an Uber home

and then figure out a way to buy a new battery when the day was done. She didn't have the energy to work on that now.

"I'll pick you up this afternoon. I'm working from home today, still looking for a place to set up my practice."

"No, really…"

"Let me help you. You're so stubborn sometimes."

She laughed and rolled her eyes. "Okay, fine. Thanks. Does five o'clock work?"

"Perfect," he said. "I'll be here."

* * *

Later that evening when they finally got home, Maree opened the front door of her apartment and stepped inside, almost tripping over something. She righted herself with a curse, then flicked on the light switch.

"Bad words, Mummy!" Sam said indignantly.

"Sorry, buddy. But what on earth?" She looked at the floor. There was a car battery sitting there with a note attached.

The note read:

I thought you could use this. Merry Christmas. Jemma let me bring it inside.
Jack xo

Maree stared at the battery. It must've cost him several hundred dollars. She wasn't sure the going rate for a battery, but it was a lot. Why was he doing this? Did he still feel bad about leaving her? She hoped he did. The way it'd all played out was something she'd never really come to terms with. It'd seemed to her at the time that he'd left because she wasn't enough for him, that there was something wrong with her. She'd been raised in a family that tore people down rather than building them up, and her self-esteem wasn't big enough to handle a rejection like the one she'd felt when Jack left after only two years of marriage without so much as an explanation.

He'd lost his brother a couple of weeks earlier. She knew he was reeling, but she hadn't known what to do to help him. He and his brother were twins. It was a whole thing—their connection, the love they shared, the way they did life together. Jack's grief was too big for her. She was lost in the depths of it. His despair overwhelmed her, and she felt unmoored. And then he was gone. He left a note telling her goodbye, but didn't give his reasons. And when she tried to call him, the phone line was disconnected. He'd run out on her without giving her a chance to fight for their marriage, and it'd torn her heart out. And when she did a pregnancy test a month later, she'd discovered that Sam was on the way. But by then, she was so angry with Jack and felt so alone in the world, she decided not to tell his family or try to track him down with the news. If he didn't want to be a part of their lives, she certainly wasn't going to force him. He had no idea that Sam was his son. And now, after so many years, she had no idea how to tell him.

Chapter Twelve

The next day, Jemma wasn't feeling any better. Dan went to work again, even though it was Sunday. She'd hoped they might lay in bed together, perhaps get some breakfast at the Black Cat, their favourite haunt. Watch the waves roll in while they ate the famous pancakes with bacon and syrup. She loved going there for brunch on a Sunday morning after church. It was one of her usual rituals. But since he had gone into the office, she didn't get up for church or brunch. Instead, she was still in her pyjamas at ten o'clock and had thrown up most of her breakfast when a bout of morning sickness hit an hour earlier.

She pulled a packet of hummus chips out of the pantry and sat at the round kitchen table.

"You doing okay?" Maree asked.

Maree and Sam sat in the living room watching cartoons together. Both wore swimsuits. Sam had a pair of goggles on top of his head, and his eyes were red-rimmed from wearing the goggles in the surf that morning.

"I'm fine," Jemma replied. "This morning sickness is kicking my butt."

Maree offered a sympathetic look. "It gets better. Hang in there."

"I hope so. Did you find the car battery Jack brought over?"

"I tripped over it on my way in last night." Maree laughed. "I can't believe he did that."

"What's it for?" Jemma asked.

"Mine went dead yesterday. He drove for us since I couldn't get it started. I mentioned that I couldn't really afford to replace it, and he must've gone and bought one after he dropped me at work."

"That was nice of him. Although I think you tripped over the old one. The new one is already in your car."

Jemma had often wondered what happened between Jack and Maree. She was always tight-lipped about it—didn't like to talk about her marriage breakdown. This gesture by Jack seemed to suggest he still cared about Maree, even if he didn't want to be married to her.

Would she and Dan end up like the two of them someday? The thought brought a lump to her throat. She didn't want that. She'd vowed to spend her life with him, and it was her dream to grow old together. But sometimes he was so difficult to understand.

"Really?" Maree asked.

Jemma nodded, crunching on a chip. "I saw him installing it."

"That's very nice of him," Maree replied, thoughtfully chewing on her lower lip. "It's just strange."

"Why?"

Maree glanced at Sam, then shuffled over to sit at the table and spoke in a hushed voice. "When he left, he changed his phone number. He never once checked on me or called to talk about the divorce. He kept his distance, even when we signed the papers. I haven't heard from him in five years. His family called sometimes. I was close with them, and they said they miss me. But those calls have become less frequent in recent years. I thought I'd never see any of them again. And now here he is, living next door, and buying me gifts." Her eyes were wide. "What do you think that means?"

At this point, Jemma was the last person in the world who could give advice about what men did or thought. She'd believed she was close enough to Dan that she could've predicted his thoughts and what he might say or do next. But lately he was acting as though he was an entirely different person from the one she'd fallen in love with.

"I have no idea. I would've said it meant he still had some kind of affection for you. But lately, I'm questioning my own judgement on everything."

"Don't do that." Maree patted her arm. "You and Dan will get through this. It's just a tumultuous time with everything that's going on."

"Thanks, honey. Hey, I'm about to call Beth in Sydney. Do you want to join?"

Maree smiled. "That would be great. I haven't spoken to her in a while."

They called Beth via video on Jemma's laptop. Jemma almost cried when she saw her pretty face. She missed having her friend close by. She could've used a few comforting words right now. Her hormones were all over the place, making her weepier than she'd usually be. She couldn't help herself.

"Hey, Beth," Jemma said. "I've got Maree here with me."

Beth grinned. "It's good to see the two of you. I miss you so much."

"We miss you as well," Maree replied.

"We do," Jemma agreed. "I could really do with a Beth hug right now."

"What's going on, sweetie?"

Jemma's throat tightened at her friend's kindness. "I have good news. I'm pregnant!"

Beth's scream shocked both Jemma and Maree. But within moments, all three of them were shouting and crying together.

"This is so exciting!"

Maree smiled. "It's wonderful. I'm glad you're telling people. I don't think I could keep it to myself for much longer."

Jemma wiped her eyes. "I've wanted to tell everyone, but it's been early. But I've passed the twelve week mark, so now it's public knowledge. We called our families last night to tell them."

"I'm so happy for you," Beth said. "Oh, I really want to be there. I have to throw you a baby shower."

"That would be amazing," Jemma said.

"Oh, but darn, I'm going to be travelling for this project at work. I'll be in Sunshine next weekend and for Christmas. Could we do it before the holiday? I know it's ridiculously early, but I'm not sure when I'll get back there again. The new year is going to be nuts."

Jemma nodded. "Next weekend would be fine. I don't want anything big. If the two of you are there, that's all I need."

"Are you okay?" Beth asked, leaning forward to scrutinise Jemma through her screen. "You look a little wiped."

"I haven't been feeling great," Jemma replied.

"She threw up this morning," Maree added. "I heard her through the bathroom wall."

"Sorry," Jemma said with a shake of her head. "I try not to be loud, but I can't really seem to help it."

"Don't be sorry. You're growing a baby. This is all part of the process. A disgusting and really annoying part, but it's a good thing. It means your hormones are doing what they're supposed to do."

"I'm glad you can put a positive spin on it," Jemma replied.

"I'm sure you'll feel better soon," Beth said.

"And ... Dan is acting strangely," Jemma added, feeling her cheeks warm. She hated to speak ill of her husband to anyone, but she needed some comfort.

"What do you mean?" Beth asked.

"We've been trying to get pregnant for so long. And when I told him, all he could think about was how it would impact the business. And he's been working ever since. I've hardly seen him."

Beth hesitated. "I'm sorry, sweetie. That must be hard. But I'm sure it doesn't mean anything. He's a man—they respond to things differently than we do. Who knows why he's acting that way? But I do know this—he loves you, and he's wanted this for a long time."

"You're right," Jemma replied, wiping her eyes again. "I have to hold on to that. I think I'm so full of hormones, it's hard for me to see straight."

"I'll be up there next weekend, and I can give you a big hug," Beth said. "It's all going to be okay."

Chapter Thirteen

That evening, Jemma watched Sam so Maree could take a run. One of the best things about rooming with her friends was the built-in babysitting. But Jemma's announcement that morning had reminded her that it was only a matter of time until she and Sam had to find somewhere else to live.

She padded down the footpath toward the beach in her joggers, then stopped at the edge of the sand to pull up her socks. There was nothing worse than the feeling of sand granules inside her socks.

She stepped onto the sand, and it moved beneath her feet, squeaking under her shoes as she picked up the pace.

Where would they go?

Seagulls squawked overhead as the heat of the day was pushed gently away by an ocean breeze.

They'd lived on their own prior to moving in with Jemma and Dan, but it'd been so hard. She'd worked full time at Sam's daycare, and the money was a little better than waitressing, since it was a forty-hour week. But now that she was enrolled at the university, she couldn't manage forty hours and look after Sam as well, so her income was much less. Would she have to give up her studies? If she did that, they'd never crawl out of this financial hole.

Hopelessness made her gut squeeze as she reached the harder sand and broke into a run. Every time she tried to do something good for them, it backfired. Nothing worked out. Life seemed to get harder and harder with every year that passed, and her natural pessimism didn't really help matters. She wished she could be one of those perky, happy people who looked at life like a bowl of different-flavoured ice creams. But it'd never been that way for her, and she couldn't pretend.

Just as she was gaining momentum, she thought she heard her name carried on the wind. She cocked her head to one side, still running, and listened. There it was again. She stopped and cupped a hand over her eyes to cut the glare as she scanned the beach.

Jack ran down the beach to meet her. Her heart skipped a beat at the sight of him, chestnut curls flopping over his forehead, bare feet slapping the sand.

"Hi," he said, puffing lightly. "I didn't think you heard me."

"Hi," she replied. "Is everything okay?"

"I know you like to run on the beach. I thought I might find you down here when I saw you leave the apartment."

Was he watching her? She crossed her arms over her chest. "Okay..."

"Sorry, that sounds stalkerish. It's not that. I was about to head out myself, and I heard your door open and close just before I came outside."

"Oh, that makes sense." She was still waiting. What did he want? She had so many things on her mind, she didn't need more. Jack was fast becoming an issue, and she wasn't sure how she was going to manage his intrusion into her life. There were things she hadn't told him. Things she regretted keeping from him. But it was too late now. And if he figured it out, he would be angry. Very angry. She was certain of that.

"We need to talk," he said.

She held her breath. "Oh? What about?"

"Can we sit?"

She nodded and followed him to the edge of the beach. They sat at the base of the dunes where the seagrass waved towards the ocean. She broke off a piece of seagrass and folded it over and over between her fingers.

"How are things?" she asked, staring at the seagrass in her hand.

He put one finger beneath her chin and gently lifted her gaze to meet his. His grey eyes were soft and full of desire. "Our kiss..."

"You said that was for closure."

"I lied."

She swallowed hard. What was he saying?

"I wanted to kiss you. It felt right."

"But we're divorced, Jack."

"I know that. It was a mistake."

Her throat filled with tears, and she couldn't speak.

He continued. "I shouldn't have left. It was immature and stupid. I was in so much pain. Jordan's death was completely out of the blue . . . it was preventable. I was angry. So angry. A drunk driver took my brother from me when he and I should've had our whole lives together. I couldn't see straight. It was too much to bear."

"You could've talked to me about it."

"I know," he replied. "But you seemed so distant. As though you didn't care..."

"I did care," she interrupted with a cry.

"Of course you did. But I couldn't see it. I was stupid. Did I say that already?" He smiled.

"You did."

He took her hand and caressed her palm with his fingers. "I need you to be honest with me. Are you really getting married?"

She shook her head. "I made that up."

"I figured, since Dan didn't know anything about a fiancé."

She huffed. "I could have a secret fiancé. He doesn't know *everything* about my life."

Jack raised both hands in surrender. "Sorry, you're right. There's probably a hidden fiancé somewhere who has never come to visit you at the apartment."

She laughed and pushed a strand of hair behind her ear. Anything to keep her hands away from his. His touch brought goose bumps down the length of her arms and along her spine.

"So ... Sam?"

It was the question she'd been dreading. He was bound to ask it. Anyone would. He'd left five years ago. Sam was almost five years old. It made sense to ask. But she'd hoped it would never come to this. She felt so much guilt and shame for hiding Sam from him all this time. Would he ever forgive her?'

"He's yours," she replied simply, looking him straight in the eyes.

Those eyes filled with pain, and he blinked. "I wasn't expecting that. He's mine?"

"Yes, he's yours. When you left, I was two months pregnant."

He looked away, his face reddening. "Did you know?"

"No, I didn't. We were grieving. There was so much turmoil. I thought I'd missed a period because of the stress. It happened to me sometimes. It wasn't really a big deal. And we weren't trying... It wasn't until after you'd left that I ran a test."

"But you never told me," he said firmly. He pressed his lips into a thin line.

She inhaled slowly. "I didn't have your number. Remember?"

"But you could've called my mum. She would've told me."

"That's true. But I was hurt, angry. You'd left me with no means of contacting you. I was scared and didn't know what to do. When the divorce papers came so quickly, I was shocked. I'd thought you would come back, that we'd face the birth and raising a child together. But you'd moved on, or so I believed."

"I didn't move on," he said numbly. "I was trying to keep my head above water."

"All I knew was that I had to be a mother on my own. And so that's what I did."

"I'm sorry," he said, looking at her with dark eyes.

"So am I," she said. "I'm not angry with you anymore. But the hurt is still there."

"I hope you understand a little more now," he said.

She nodded. "I think I get it. I know you two were very close. And it was a shock to all of us."

"I should've leaned on you."

"I should've given you the chance," she replied softly.

"So, what about us? What about now?" he asked with a swallow.

She sighed. "There is no 'us.' But you can meet Sam again. I'll tell him. Just give me a little time."

"We'll be friends."

"And co-parents," she agreed.

He nodded, his face stern. "Okay. It's a start."

Chapter Fourteen

The Aurora Boutique Inn rose against the backdrop of she-oaks and pandanus. Behind the inn, the sun bore down on a long beach, the white sand sparkling beneath its rays. Gwen Prince stood in front of the newly renovated structure with her hands on her hips, surveying the sagging eaves on one side with a frown on her face.

"That's not good," she said beneath her breath. She'd just paid six figures to have this inn renovated to the highest standards, and now one eve was hanging too low. There was a leak inside the inn as well, which she'd traced to the sagging eve. And now she had a very unhappy guest with a suitcase full of soggy clothing.

She picked up her phone and called Mark, the contractor who'd managed the renovation. "Mark, it's Gwen."

"Hi, Gwen. How are you?" he asked in a warm voice.

"I'm well, thank you. But I've got an issue at the inn."

By the time she'd described the issue to him, the eve had sunk lower still. And when she hung up the phone, it made a creaking sound and looked as though it might break.

"That's *definitely* not good," she repeated with a sigh.

Mark was on his way. There was nothing more she could do other than hope for the best.

She hurried inside. It was almost time for the dinner service, and she still had a lot to do before then. The inn's foyer was decorated with holly and mistletoe. The large Christmas tree that she'd also used the previous year was sparkling with Christmas lights, and soft Christmas carols floated through the air.

Maree, one of the servers from the restaurant, sat at the bottom of the staircase crying. Gwen stopped her headlong dash toward her office, spun on her heel, and hurried to where Maree sat.

"Maree, what's wrong? What happened?"

Her blonde hair was pulled back into a ponytail, but strands fell around her cheeks. She pressed her palms to her eyes and sniffed before standing.

"Nothing, sorry. I'm fine. I promise, I wasn't there long."

"It's okay. I'm not mad—I'm worried about you."

Maree sniffled again. "I twisted my ankle. It's no big deal."

"What are you doing in here? Are you looking for someone?"

Maree shook her head. "Just a quiet place to sit. This was the closest place I could hobble to." She gave a lopsided smile.

"Do you need to go home?"

Maree looked stricken. "No, really, I'm fine. I don't want to go home. I need this shift."

Gwen patted her arm. "You let me know then, okay? If you've got to go home, that's perfectly fine. We'll figure it out."

Maree hobbled back into the restaurant, and Gwen watched her with concern. She would have to find something else for Maree to do other than wait tables. She couldn't do that with a twisted ankle. She sighed—if she couldn't find anyone else on such short notice, she'd have to wait tables again. And she was already having to cover for Francesca, who was out sick. She'd have to manage the inn *and* wait tables. She could be in two places at once, couldn't she? It was totally doable.

She immediately returned to her office to work on the accounts. The inn was quiet at first, but guests soon made their way downstairs to the restaurant or in the direction of town for dinner. They were a small establishment, and today, they only had forty guests. But it was enough to keep her and her staff very busy. They'd have more for dinner at the restaurant—word had gotten out about the bistro's delicious French cuisine, and people came from far and wide. She tried to keep tables open for guests, but they had to book ahead of time.

"Hello?" A man's voice broke through her concentration. Mark rapped his knuckles against her open door with a smile. "Busy?"

She grinned. "Always busy, but never too busy for you."

"Can I come in?"

"Please take a seat. I'll be with you in a moment. I'm just finishing up some accounting."

He groaned. "The bane of my existence."

"I know exactly what you mean," she replied with a few clicks of the mouse. Then she stood to her feet. "Thanks for coming so quickly. I called about the leak, and I found a sagging eve. I think they're connected."

"That's probably a good bet." He stood as well and waved a hand for her to lead the way.

She hurried out of the office with him close behind. "Do you have plans for Christmas?"

"I'm spending Christmas Eve at the McLintock Stables. We're putting on a meal and a dance for the kids. The horses will be dressed up and get lots of grooming. We do it every year. It's fun."

"That sounds lovely."

"And then, for Christmas Day, I'll be at my son's house. He has a swimming pool, which seems to be the main criteria for where to host Christmas Day now that the grandchildren are at that age." He chuckled.

She nodded. "These kids are so spoiled, aren't they?" She laughed. "A pool is nice, for sure. That and space. I have a pool at my unit but don't have enough space for the entire family. So, we'll be going to Brandon's again this year. I'm still getting used to the fact that I'm not hosting, but it's nice not to have to do all that work. Especially now that I'm running the Aurora."

"I really enjoyed spending time with you at the riding school."

"Me too," she replied, suddenly feeling self-conscious. She liked him. More than she was even willing to admit to herself. She didn't trust her own judgement anymore, but he was different to her ex-husband. He was kind, gentle and thoughtful. He spent his spare time teaching disabled children to ride —that was nothing like Duncan, who spent most of his time looking for the next dollar. Maybe she should give him a chance, although it was difficult for her to open up her heart again.

"We should do something else soon. How do you feel about bushwalking?"

She laughed. "I feel pretty good about bushwalking."

"Great. How about next Saturday? We could walk to this waterfall that I love. It's got a beautiful deep pool of water at the base. We could have a swim, maybe take some lunch."

It sounded like a dream come true. "I'd love that."

Chapter Fifteen

Jemma hadn't done any of her usual traditions for Christmas yet. And now that she knew she was pregnant and the throwing up seemed to have abated for a few minutes, she decided it was time. She stood in the kitchen, thumbing through a recipe book, and then stopped to look around at the decorations in their small apartment. Each item brought back memories of their first Christmases together as a married couple. She'd carefully curated a series of cute, kitschy decorations that involved Santa in varying formats and reindeer of all kinds.

They didn't have much space in the apartment, and they'd never had much spare money on hand, so the décor was sparse. But she'd lovingly selected these few items to match their personality and the space—a beachside apartment—as best she could. One of the Santas wore board shorts and had a surfboard beneath his arm.

She was alone in the house again and found she enjoyed the solitude. She hadn't had much of that in recent years, as she was always working. But since her morning sickness—all day sickness, really—had taken hold, she'd been spending more time at home getting ready for the baby and resting. She'd hoped the second trimester would be better, but so far, it wasn't looking good. Maybe during the final few months, she'd be able to keep some food down.

She pulled a bowl out of the cupboard and began to measure out the ingredients for gingerbread. When she was almost finished mixing the flour, sugar, and spices together, the front door opened, and Dan stepped through. His normally smooth brown hair was dishevelled, and his tie was loosened around his neck. He set his briefcase on the coffee table and bent to kiss her.

"Hey, honey. What are you making?"

"Gingerbread," she said. "Merry Christmas."

He smiled wearily. "You too. I'm getting something to drink. You want anything?"

"No, thanks. You're home early." She watched him reach for a glass.

He filled it with water and downed it in three gulps, then sighed. "I've got to pack. I'm going away tomorrow."

"Going away? Where?" She leaned against the bench and crossed her arms.

"There's a conference on the Gold Coast, and I'm going to network for a few days. It'll be good for the business."

"Oh, okay. I didn't know about it."

He leaned forward to stare into the fridge. "I only found out about it this morning. It sounds like a great opportunity."

"It's almost Christmas. How long will you be gone?"

"Only until the weekend. I've cancelled all the appointments for the rest of the week. You should relax. Do something fun."

"Something fun? I was hoping we could do some Christmas things together. Maybe drive around and look at Christmas lights. Or have some people over for eggnog. I'm making gingerbread. We could hand it out to the neighbours. I bought these cute little red bags..."

He huffed. "I'm far too tired to entertain or visit neighbours. Don't you realise how much I have going on right now? I've got to focus. I have work to do."

She tried not to show how upset his words made her feel, and she didn't understand the urgency. It would be Christmas soon. They needed to take a break. It'd been a long and busy year. All she wanted was to celebrate Christmas with all her favourite traditions and then snuggle on the couch with her husband and sip ginger ale. She was exhausted, sick, and in desperate need of comfort. But Dan didn't seem to realise any of that. And she didn't want to fight. Not again. So she kept her thoughts to herself.

"I get it. I'm sure you'll have a great time at the conference."

Chapter Sixteen

Jack's first official catch-up with Sam happened without incident. It was a normal Thursday, and Sam had spent the day at daycare while Maree worked at the inn. She'd bandaged up her injured ankle, and the shift had gone relatively smoothly. About a hundred people asked her why she was hobbling, but it was fine. She made light of the situation. But the truth was, she'd twisted her ankle because she was mooning about the Jack situation and the fact she now had to share parenting with him.

She knew it was selfish of her. He deserved to know his son, if that was what he wanted. And Sam certainly deserved to have a relationship with his own father. But for the past five years, it'd just been the two of them against the world. She'd made every choice in Sam's life. When he was allowed to watch television. Which cereal would be best for his breakfast. What colour his bed sheets would be. And now, she would have to share that responsibility. Jack would be part of her life forever. And even though she knew it was a good thing—for her and for Sam—she'd been crying quietly at the inn, when she should've been working, and she'd stumbled and injured herself.

Instead of continuing to feel sorry for herself, she went home that evening and texted Jack to set up a meeting between him and Sam. And after that, she felt much better. She was resigned to it. And maybe things would turn out for the best. Perhaps Jack could contribute something to Sam's life. And she might even get to take an evening off every now and then if Jack would watch him, although it would be a little while before they would get to that stage.

She made Sam a chocolate milkshake, and then there was a knock at the door. When she opened it, Jack stood there holding a large yellow digger in one hand. He looked awkward and nervous. She'd never seen him like that before. She led the way to the kitchen, where Sam sat at the table. He had a milk moustache.

"Sam, this is Jack. You remember Jack?"

"From the car park," Sam said. "He has a big truck."

"That's right. We talked about him last night. He's your father." Saying the words made her throat constrict.

Sam nodded, studying Jack through narrowed eyes. "You don't look like me."

"I think we have a few similarities," Jack replied, sitting across from Sam.

"Can I get you a drink?" Maree asked. She felt strained. This had to go well, but she couldn't control it.

"A milkshake sounds great."

As she fixed the milkshake, she watched Jack and Sam out of the corner of her eye. They chatted together, at first with stilted conversation. But soon, they moved to the living room floor, where Sam tried out the digger on his pile of blocks. And in no time, they were playing easily, building a Lego fort to see if the digger could knock it down.

When it was time for Sam's bath, Jack told him goodbye

and said he'd see him again soon. Maree was surprised by the look on Sam's face. He had connected with Jack in a way she hadn't expected for their first meeting. And then he threw his arms around Jack's legs to embrace him before running to the bathroom.

"Thanks for letting me spend time with him," Jack said. "He's a great kid. You've done well with him."

"You're welcome. You're committed now. I hope you realise that."

"I know."

"He's going to rely on you."

"I know, Maree." Jack shook his head. "I'll be here. I promise."

"Okay. Thanks. It means a lot."

"I wish I could've seen him…"

"I wish that too," Maree interrupted. "But we can't go back."

"You're right—I shouldn't dwell on it. We should try to have a good relationship now. Since we're co-parents."

"I think that makes a lot of sense."

He shoved his hands into his pockets. "On that note, are you busy later?"

She smiled. "I don't have anything planned. Jemma is home, so I thought I might go for a walk or something. I don't get a lot of time to myself."

"That sounds nice. Or you could come over to my apartment and watch *Die Hard* with me."

She laughed. "You know that's my favourite Christmas movie."

"I haven't forgotten." His eyes sparkled. "I have popcorn."

"Okay, that sounds good. I'll bring wine."

* * *

It'd been years since Maree had watched *Die Hard* in the lead-up to Christmas. That was something she and Jack had done when they were married, and she'd tried to put those memories behind her. But now she felt as though she could finally move on. Seeing Jack again had given her the chance to forgive him and let go of what remained from the hurt and pain she'd been holding on to.

Jack was in the living room working on getting the movie onto the screen of his very large television set.

"I'll pour the wine," she said as she headed for the kitchen. She foraged around his kitchen and found glasses. No wine glass, but water glasses would suffice. She poured the Chardonnay, and then called out, "Is the popcorn ready? Or do you want me to throw it in the microwave?"

"It's ready, but there's a dip in the fridge if you have a spare hand."

She couldn't carry dip plus two glasses, so she set the glasses on the coffee table first and went back for the dip. One glance told her it was his famous Mexican layer dip, so she grabbed the packet of chips she could see and carried them out as well.

"I love your dip," she said, eying it as she set it down on the table beside the wine glasses.

He laughed. "I know you do."

Was he trying to impress her? He'd remembered her favourite movie and made the dip she loved. She couldn't help being a little moved, although she didn't want to get carried away by emotion. She had to keep her distance. They shared a son. It was important to keep his life stable. And falling for Jack again would definitely not do that. He might leave at the drop of a hat, and then where would they be?

She settled down onto the couch and removed the lid from the dip.

Jack sat beside her and pressed play on the movie. He raised his glass toward her. "Thanks for the wine."

"No worries," she said, clinking her own glass against his.

"To our future together," he said.

She studied his grey eyes, which seemed so innocent, so unassuming. Did he know what he was doing, or was it all a coincidence? "To the future," she said, intentionally altering his words.

They each drank, then got comfortable as the movie began to play.

After a few minutes, Jack spoke. "I wanted to call you when the Broncos won."

She spun to face him, eyes wide. "I wanted to call you too, but I didn't have your number. Can you believe it?"

He laughed. "I was so chuffed. I jumped up and down and screamed, looked for you to high-five, and of course, you weren't there."

"We went to so many games, and they were on such an awful losing streak. To win the grand final the following year was just ... argh!"

"I know, and we missed it. I was at a business function having drinks with colleagues and saw it on a muted screen hanging beside the bar."

"I was at home with Sam. I couldn't scream because he fell asleep right at kickoff."

They both laughed. Maree buzzed with the happiness of reconnecting with Jack. He'd been her best friend. They'd shared so much of their lives together. She'd forgotten how good it was just to be with him, to talk and laugh, to have fun. He'd always been her favourite person. Until Sam came along, of course. And without Jack there, she'd leaned more heavily on Sam for companionship than she probably should've, but it'd only been the two of them for so long. She didn't know how to let anyone else into her life.

Chapter Seventeen

It was the day of Jemma's baby shower, and Dan still hadn't returned from the Gold Coast. He'd promised her he would be back by Saturday. But the previous evening, he'd called to say he wanted to stay for the weekend. The conference was still going, and he was getting a lot of good contacts out of it. She'd agreed he should stay, of course. It was work; it was necessary. But it didn't help her feel any better about it.

"Do you need me to drive you to the party?" Maree asked, poking her head out of the bathroom door as Jemma walked down the hallway.

"That would be great. Thanks. I'm feeling a little better after breakfast, but I was so ill this morning."

"You're having such a rough go of it," Maree said, her face drawn with empathy. "Let's hope it means that baby is thriving in there."

"I don't know how he or she can thrive without any nutrients."

Maree disappeared back into the bathroom, where she was curling her hair. "Oh, don't worry. They suck the nutrients they need right out of you."

"That sounds lovely," Jemma said with a laugh.

She finished applying her makeup seated at her vanity, and then checked her reflection in the mirror. Her stomach was still almost entirely flat. There was a little roundness to it, but that was probably bloating from how unwell she felt. The doctor assured her it would pop out after twenty weeks, so before long, her body would change entirely. She couldn't imagine it. But she was looking forward to getting further into the pregnancy and hopefully feeling better.

"I have to pick Beth up from the airport at ten. Then we'll go right to the shower at her mother's unit by the beach. Have you seen it?"

Maree joined her in the bedroom and sat on her bed. "No, I haven't been there."

"It's lovely. Not very big, but nice."

"Is Gwen doing all the decorations?"

"Decorations, food, all of it. She's so thoughtful. Beth couldn't put it together since she's not here. But she promised to help clean up afterward."

"I wish I had a mother like that," Maree said with a wistful sigh. "I can't imagine mine being so supportive."

"Have you spoken to your parents recently?"

"No, not for a while, although I'll call them at Christmas. They don't really seem to mind if I don't call, and when I do, they're often busy and can't talk long. Mum and my stepfather haven't been to see Sam in about six months. They've decided to travel around Australia in an RV, and they don't have time to stop in to see us in Sunshine. It's out of their way, apparently."

"I'm sorry to hear that," Jemma said. "Mine do make the effort. But unfortunately, we don't see them very often. Maybe they'll come up more frequently once the baby is born."

"That would be nice."

Jemma searched her closet for a purse that would match

the purple print dress she wore. A silver one would do. She threw her wallet, keys, and lip balm inside, and then slipped her feet into silver flats.

"I've been meaning to talk to you about something," Maree said.

Jemma joined her on the edge of the bed. "Oh? What is it?"

Maree cleared her throat. "With the baby coming, I assume Sam and I will have to find a place to go."

Jemma hadn't wanted to have this conversation. She'd put it off and avoided raising it. But it seemed they both knew it was a topic in need of discussion. "I don't want you to leave, but..."

"But you need the space," Maree finished her sentence for her.

"Right, we need the space. I'm sorry, honey."

"It's fine. We've got time to look for somewhere new to live."

"You've got plenty of time. The baby will probably live in our bedroom in a bassinet for the first few months."

"No, it's okay. I want to be moved out before the little one gets here. You two need your space, and this will be a really special time for you to share. I wish I'd had that with Jack." Maree's eyes glistened, and she bent her head to stare at the carpet.

Jemma rested a hand on her arm. "I know you do. I still can't believe he left like that. But he's a good guy with a good heart. If he left, it was because he felt he had no other option. And he didn't know about Sam."

"I never asked—did Dan stay in touch with him?" Maree asked, her gaze finding Jemma's.

She shook her head. "He didn't tell anyone where he was. It was only recently that he got back in touch with us. I would've told you if we'd known. And I didn't think it was my place to tell him about Sam."

"Thanks. I'm glad I got to tell him myself."

"I'm glad you did too. It was the right thing. He'll be a good dad."

"I know he will. If he can manage to stick around..." Maree rolled her eyes.

Jemma laughed. "I think he will. He's older and more mature. He's changed."

"He *does* seem different," Maree mused. "But I suppose we'll have to wait and see."

The baby shower was sweet, and Jemma was very touched by how much effort had been made. Gwen had decorated her unit with all sorts of sweet baby décor—all in a delightful yellow, since they didn't know yet what the sex of the baby would be. There were games, although not many, as Jemma had assured Gwen ahead of time that she wasn't much for games.

They did have a guessing game over the contents of a series of nappies. Squashed Snickers bar, or Vegemite, peanut butter or chocolate bar? It was a lot of fun, and all of the women present were doubled over in laughter when Maree gagged at the sight of chocolate dripping from one onto the floor.

After the party was over, Beth, Maree, and Jemma helped Gwen to clean up. Jemma was tired but otherwise felt pretty good. She'd managed to snack consistently for the past two hours and so didn't feel sick.

"How are you going in Dee Why?" Jemma asked Beth.

Beth swept the floor. "It's great. I've found an amazing job, which I love. I'm working on a complete rebrand for a large food company. And they're wonderful to work with. My flat is close to work, so I can catch the train and then walk the rest of the way. Plus, I'm close to the beach, which you know I can't live without."

"And what about Damien? How are things with him? The man you spent fifteen years waiting for…" Jemma laughed. "Your story is so romantic, I almost can't stand it."

Beth blushed. "Things with Damien are great. We're dating, spending time together. We usually do something outdoors on the weekend, like go surfing or bushwalking. We enjoy a lot of the same activities. We have so much in common. It's like no relationship I've ever had before. That connection we felt on the first New Year's Eve when we were kids was a sign. We have a chemistry that is hard to deny. And it's only growing the more time we spend together."

"Are you in love?" Maree asked.

Beth nodded. "Definitely—head over heels." She grinned. "It's wonderful."

"Should we expect wedding bells soon?"

"I don't know if it'll be soon, but I know he's the one. And he feels the same way. We've talked about it. I can see us getting engaged sometime in the next year."

Jemma's heart swelled. She loved to see her friend find happiness. "I'm thrilled. But I'd always hoped you'd get married and live here on the island. I suppose you'll be down south."

"Who knows what the future holds?" Beth said as she finished sweeping. "But for now, we'll be staying put since Damien's business is there."

"I'll have to visit you, that's all," Jemma replied.

"I'll come too. Now that Sam has Jack in his life, I might even get to have a weekend away sometime," Maree said wistfully. "Not soon, since they have to get to know one another. But I can imagine it happening, and that's almost as good as actually doing it."

"Anticipation is everything," Jemma agreed.

"I hope you visit all the time," Beth said. "I miss you both. And I miss Mum, too." She glanced at Gwen, who'd just walked into the room with an armful of wrapping paper to take out to the bin.

"I miss you too, honey. But I'm so happy you're doing well. That's all a mother wants for her daughter. To be happy and thriving in life. It gives me so much peace."

"Thanks, Mum." She put an arm around Gwen's shoulders and squeezed.

"Thank you for the baby shower," Jemma said to Gwen. "It means a lot. I know how busy you are with the inn and restaurant."

Gwen smiled. "I'm happy to do it. This is the stuff I enjoy. And work is getting a little less intense. I think I've got most things covered. Thankfully, the leaking roof has been fixed. And Mark even took a look around and made sure there was nothing else to cause me any trouble. Apparently a tree branch hit the eve during a storm, and none of us realised since the branch ended up on the ground."

"There's so much to think about," Beth said with a nod at her mother. "But you're doing great."

"It's never-ending. And I love it. I'd better take this outside before my arms fall off," Gwen said with a grunt.

After she left, Jemma slumped onto the couch with a sigh. "I have to get off my feet. I'm so tired these days."

"Pregnancy must feel so strange," Beth said, joining her. She leaned a head on Jemma's shoulder.

"It is very strange, but pretty great. I feel like my body isn't my own any longer. And I'm sick all the time. I am definitely looking forward to having the baby in my arms and my body back."

Maree perched on the arm of the couch. "You look great, though. Doesn't she?"

"She's amazing, as always," Beth said. "You two are so lucky that you get to live together. I'm living by myself in a tiny flat. It's in a great location, but the rent is so expensive."

"Maybe you should find a roommate," Maree suggested.

"I should, but it's hard when you don't really know anyone. I've made a few friends at work now, though. And I've joined a walking group on the weekends for when Damien's working."

"It takes time to establish yourself in a new place and develop those relationships," Jemma said.

"I'm getting there," Beth replied. "Now, where is that cake? I need another piece. It was divine."

"I'll get it for you. Don't move," Maree said. "Do you want a piece, Jemma?"

"Yes, please."

Maree brought three slices of cake and forks to eat it with. The three of them sat on the couch, chatting about life and love while they ate. Jemma soaked it all in, aware that it wouldn't last long, and Beth would be gone again soon. She thought about all the years ahead when she would be a mother and everything in her life would be different, including her friendships. And she couldn't help feeling a little nervous but excited at the prospect.

Chapter Eighteen

The next day, Jemma met Beth for a coffee at the Black Cat. It was like old times, and she was feeling rather emotional, her hormones in full swing. When she embraced her friend, tears sprang into her eyes. She wiped them away before she sat.

"Oh, honey, are you okay?" Beth asked.

"I'm fine. I miss you, that's all. And it's so nice to have you here. I really appreciate that you threw me the baby shower."

"You're welcome. I wish I could've done more. But life is so hectic right now."

"I know how it is," Jemma replied.

They ordered drinks and muffins. Jemma couldn't help but think about all the conversations they'd usually have about her pregnancy and life, but they didn't because it would've had to happen over the phone. And Jemma had never been great at phone conversations.

"How are things with you and Dan? He must be thrilled about the baby," Beth said as she sipped her cappuccino.

Jemma stared into her hot chocolate, stirring it slowly. "I thought he would be too."

"Oh, no. What happened?"

Jemma met her friend's gaze. "He hasn't stopped working since I told him. He's worried about me pulling back, losing clients, maybe losing business. I don't think that will happen. I'm sure they'll be more than happy to work with him, but he's so stressed about it. It makes me feel as though he cares more about how much money I bring in than who I am or our growing family." She bit back the tears and took a mouthful of hot chocolate, scalding her tongue.

"I'm sure that's not true. He was so looking forward to having a baby."

"I know, but it's been very hard for me. I want him to be there, to hold me, to tell me everything's going to be okay. Not to argue with me about how it will all fall apart without me working." She sighed. "I don't know what to do. But I feel very alone."

"Have you spoken to him about it?"

"Not really. I haven't had a chance. He's on the Gold Coast at a conference right now. And when he's home, he isn't there—he's at the office or out meeting with clients. It's like we're waving at each other as we pass by."

"It's the restaurant all over again," Beth replied.

Jemma's gut clenched. "What do you mean?"

"He did the same thing when the two of you bought that little restaurant. Remember? He was absolutely consumed with supplies and vendors, renovating and seating numbers."

"You're right." Jemma leaned back in her chair. It was the same thing. Why hadn't she seen that?

"You were both too inexperienced to make it work. It wasn't your fault. You tried, and personally, I liked the place. But most restaurants fail, and he didn't cope with that."

"Are you inferring that the real estate business will fail too?"

"Of course not." Beth leaned forward to squeeze her hand. "I'm saying, this is how he copes with anxiety."

"He's anxious about the baby? Why would he be anxious? He doesn't have to carry it inside him for nine months and then squeeze it out."

Beth laughed. "No, he can't control that, so he's controlling what he can."

"You think that's what it is?"

Beth nodded. "At least, I sure hope so. And knowing him as well as I do, yes, I think that's what's going on. He's afraid that he's going to fail you and the baby, and he's doing what he can to make sure that doesn't happen."

"I really wish he'd use his words to express himself," Jemma groaned.

"See, you're gonna be a great mum." Beth laughed.

Just then, Maree arrived breathless and in a hurry. She embraced both of the women then sat in a huff, sweat beading on her forehead. "It's too hot for this." She fanned herself. "What are we drinking? Oh, dear. I'm getting an iced coffee."

Maree ordered her drink then leaned back in her chair. "This week has been something else."

"What's going on?"

"I injured myself at work, so I'm hobbling everywhere."

"What happened?" Beth asked, concern etched across her pretty face.

"I was thinking about Jack..."

"Ooooh," Jemma said with a smug look. "That sounds promising."

"What have I missed?" Beth asked.

Maree inhaled a slow breath. "Jack's moved in across the hall from us. And he knows about Sam."

"Wow. That's big news." Beth's eyes widened.

"Yep. And he wants to spend time with us, hang out, get to know Sam."

"They had a movie date at his flat," Jemma added with a wink.

"It wasn't a date. We spent some time together watching my favourite Christmas movie."

"And he got all her favourite foods and wine. It was very romantic." Jemma laughed.

Maree's cheeks flamed. "I don't think he was trying to be romantic. Thoughtful, maybe."

"It sounds romantic to me," Beth replied.

"So, what does it mean? That's the question you should be asking," Jemma added.

The waitress arrived with her drink, and Maree hesitated until she was gone. "I don't know. I'm very confused. He seemingly wants to have a relationship of some kind—maybe friendship. And then there was the kiss..."

"What?" Beth exclaimed.

"What kiss?" Jemma asked, gaping. "You never said anything about a kiss."

Maree grimaced. "Oh, yeah, that's right. You don't know about that. At your hens party, he suggested we have a final kiss... you know, for closure."

Beth whooped.

Jemma burst out laughing. "Closure? Kissing is not what you do when you want closure. Not even close."

"He's still in love with you," Beth said.

Maree shook her head vehemently. "No, definitely not. It was just a kiss. A great kiss—an earth-shattering one, even. But his kisses were always like that...although he did say leaving was his biggest regret." Her body warmed thinking about it.

"An earth-shattering kiss, and you don't know whether he's still in love with you? Plus he regrets leaving. Sounds like you're in denial." Beth crossed her arms.

"Definitely," Jemma agreed.

Maree forced a smile onto her face. Were they right? Was it

obvious? But she could never tell with Jack. He hid his feelings from her before—maybe he was doing the same thing again. He talked about regret as though he wanted more, but he'd said he loved her in the past and then he'd left. She couldn't trust him with her heart. It hurt too much when he walked away.

Chapter Nineteen

Maree stood in front of the small Christmas tree in the living room staring at the empty floor beneath the tree. Christmas was not far away, and she still didn't have much for Sam. She'd bought a couple of Matchbox cars and a candy bar, but what he really wanted was a bike with training wheels. She'd looked at all the bikes in the various shops close by, but they were out of her price range. She still had to pay rent this month and buy food. Plus with her university fees coming due around the same time, she wasn't going to have anything left over for gifts.

She'd thought about asking her parents, but they were travelling. And besides, they'd never shown much interest in Sam. When she'd asked for help in the past, they'd muttered something about chickens coming home to roost, as though she'd brought this situation on herself. They'd never liked that she and Jack had married so young and hadn't supported her decision at the time. Now they acted smug whenever she shared her troubles with them, so she'd stopped saying anything. When she spoke to them these days, she pretended everything was fine and she was thriving. It was the best way to maintain a relationship with them.

But it wouldn't fix the Christmas situation.

She smoothed the front of her red silk dress and pushed a stray ringlet behind one ear. Sam was being watched by a friend from work today because it was Emily and Aaron's wedding. She was excited to get out of the flat and spend some fun time with other adults. Plus, she adored Emily and Aaron. They were the perfect couple—both gentle, kind, and with eyes only for one another. She was happy for them and was looking forward to the celebration.

There was one issue, though, that made her stomach stir with nerves—Jack had asked if she would go with him as his date. He hadn't simply offered to give her a lift, since she could've driven with Jemma and Dan, who'd left ten minutes ago. He'd been clear—it was a date. He wanted her to attend with him. And she'd weakly agreed, unable to say no to him. Now her stomach was clenched into a knot, and she was doing her best not to nervously chew on a fingernail and ruin her red polish.

When he knocked on the door, she inhaled a gasp of air, then shook her head with resolve and went to answer it. He looked so handsome in his suit, hair slicked back. His grey eyes sparkled as his gaze brushed over her, taking in her knee-length dress and stiletto heels.

He whistled. "You look amazing."

"Thanks. You do too."

He reached for her hand and took it in his. "Ready to go?"

"Let's go."

* * *

The wedding was at the Aurora Boutique Inn and Bistro. The inn looked immaculate. Inside was decorated for Christmas, with an enormous tree that towered over beautifully wrapped gifts. Maree was grateful not to be working, but there as a guest.

Emily seemed to have embraced the Christmas theme, adorning the place with red and gold. Guests dressed in red, gold, and black milled about. Maree tried to ignore the fact that Jack had taken her hand at the valet stand and walked with her, hand in hand, into the inn. If she thought about it too much, her heart raced, and she didn't want to head back down that path. But how could she get out of it now? She'd gone along with it so far and hadn't pulled away. She wasn't sure what to do.

She loved him. She was willing to admit that. She'd never stopped loving him. But she didn't trust him. He wasn't reliable. And her heart couldn't take another abandonment. She pulled her hand slowly out of his and picked up a glass of champagne from the tray of a passing waiter, and then held the drink aloft. "Mmm, champagne."

Jack smiled, but she could sense his disappointment. She wished she could read his thoughts. What was he intending? Did he want them to be a family again? If not, he was teasing her, and she couldn't imagine him being so cruel. He was a kind man. Always had been, even as a boy. The abandonment had been totally out of character, which was why she was so blindsided by it. Looking back, she should've suspected something was wrong. He'd lost his twin brother suddenly, and he was in mourning. But it was more than that. He wasn't pulling out of it—he didn't cope. She couldn't see the warning signs at the time, but now that she was older with more life experience behind her, she realised he'd been drowning. That he didn't know how to manage the situation he found himself in. And his family had been in just as much pain, so they couldn't help him either.

Just then, someone tapped a glass with a spoon and called

for everyone to go out to the back garden for the ceremony. It was time. Maree set her drink down on an empty tray and linked her arm through Jack's.

Jemma and Dan were nowhere to be seen. They were in the wedding party, and no doubt locked in a room somewhere getting ready for the ceremony. She and Jack went to find seats on the white plastic folding chairs that were lined up in front of a vine-clad gazebo. The vine was flowering, white against the dark green of the leaves. There was white tulle tied to each of the chairs, and a white carpet ran down the centre aisle. Beautiful arrays of Australian wildflowers sat on either side of the altar, and a man in a black suit stood behind it, smiling magnanimously to everyone taking seats.

Jack sat beside her. She felt his eyes on her. She looked at him, and he gave her a curious look as he leaned in to whisper, "Are you okay?"

She nodded. "I'm ok."

"You seem to have something on your mind."

"I do, but now isn't the time to talk about it."

"Later, then?"

"Later would be good." She offered him a wan smile. It was the best she could do. She drew a deep breath as Aaron and his best man, Dan, took their place up front, and a harpist began to play.

As first, Jemma, then Emily walked down the aisle, dressed beautifully in a long, fitted silk gown with a matching long veil, and clinging to Tristan's arm.

Tears sprang to Maree's eyes as she exchanged a glance and smile with her friend. Emily's own eyes shone with joy.

The ceremony was moving. The couple said their own vows, which were filled with love and sincerity—so much so that Maree found it hard to keep the tears at bay. She looked up at Jack after the vows were done, and he met her gaze with an intensity of yearning that took her breath away.

The couple walked down the aisle again as husband and wife, greeting family and friends. Maree hurried to kiss Emily on the cheek.

"It was beautiful. Congratulations," she whispered.

Emily grinned. "Thank you."

"Your dress is divine."

"I love it too," Emily said. "I wish I could wear it again."

Emily, Aaron, and the wedding party left to take photographs on the beach while everyone else filtered into the bistro. There was a section set aside for dancing. A DJ played music in the corner. The rest of the restaurant was decorated with native wildflowers, white tulle, and large, round tables with white tablecloths.

"Can I get you a drink?" Jack asked.

"Thank you. That would be great."

He soon returned with a beer and a glass of Chardonnay. They found their places at a table filled with people they didn't know.

After a moment of silence, Jack turned to her. "Thanks for letting me get to know Sam."

"I'm glad the two of you can have a relationship."

"I understand why you didn't say anything before now."

"Really?"

"Yeah, I left you. I hurt you. And you didn't know how to reach me. I get it."

"I could've made an effort," she said, the guilt eating at her.

"I wish you had. But I'm all saying is... I understand."

"Thank you. I was scared, I guess."

"Scared of what?"

"That you'd want to be a part of his life. That it would change everything. I'd lose him ... like I lost you."

He leaned back in his chair to study her. "I'm sorry. I wish I could..."

"Don't," she said, holding a finger to his lips. "Let's not talk about it now."

He smiled. "Ok."

Chapter Twenty

Jemma watched as the photographer squatted in the sand to get the perfect shot of Emily and Aaron. It'd been a lovely wedding, and she was so grateful to be part of it. But she was getting tired. And hungry too, which meant the nausea was returning with a vengeance. She opened her clutch and fossicked around, looking for something to eat. She'd already eaten the protein bar she'd stashed in the purse that morning, but she needed something more. Surely they should've thought about the wedding party needing to eat at some point. She pictured the rest of the guests chowing down on finger food at the reception, and her stomach growled.

"Was that your stomach?" Dan asked, his eyebrows arched high.

She laughed. "Yes, I'm starving. I haven't had anything but that protein bar since this whole thing began. I might throw up on your shoes."

"I still don't get how being hungry makes you sick, but okay. I'll see if I can find something."

He hurried up the beach in the direction of the inn and soon returned with a plate full of finger foods—crostini with mozzarella and basil pesto, fried baby squid, and freshly baked bread dipped in olive oil and vinegar.

She took a piece of bread and bit into it with a groan. "Bless you," she said.

He smiled. "You really are hungry."

"You have no idea. I'm apparently eating for ten. It's the only thing that keeps me from being sick all of the time. I'm going to be the size of a house before this is over."

He wrapped an arm around her waist and squeezed. "You'll still be as gorgeous as ever."

Her throat tightened. "That's the nicest thing you've said to me in ages."

"Really? I think it all the time."

"I wish you'd say things like that a little more often. I need it, you know."

"Okay, I'll try to do that." He looked at her with questions in his eyes. "You want a drink?"

"I'd love one."

He started back towards the inn. "Won't be long."

* * *

After they were finished with photos, the wedding party returned to the inn to join the party. The bistro was packed with wedding guests, and many were dancing when they walked in. The DJ stopped the music to announce the newly married couple. Jemma and Dan found their seats at the lead table, then watched as Emily and Aaron moved around the room talking to people.

Jemma was glad to get off her feet. The fatigue especially hit her at the end of a long day, and this one had been particularly exhausting, since she'd hardly slept. Nerves about the wedding had bled into anxiety about the baby and her marriage, and then she'd lain awake staring at the ceiling for hours while Dan snored next to her.

"What are you thinking about?" he asked.

She sighed. "Us, the baby, this wedding. It's beautiful."

"Yeah, they're great together. I'm happy for them."

"Do you remember our wedding?"

"Of course I do. We were blissfully happy."

She recalled the sweetness of their love, the way he'd looked at her as she walked down the aisle, the way they'd danced together for the first time as husband and wife. She'd had so many dreams for how their life would be. But years of trying to have a baby had worn on them. Would they ever get back to that place again?

"We were happy. Weren't we?"

"We still are." He looked at her with concern. "You're happy ... right?"

"Of course." She leaned into him, not wanting to spoil the moment with complaints. And what was there to complain about, really? She had a husband who loved her and worked hard to provide for them. She should be grateful. But still, she wished that connection they'd shared in the early years was still there. That he couldn't stand to be away from her and loved spending every spare moment in her presence. That he couldn't get enough of her. The adoration had been addicting. And now it was gone. Or at the very least, subdued. Would their relationship survive having a baby and the stress that would bring into their lives?

"I'm going to dance," he said, rising to his feet suddenly.

He was gone before she could object. He hadn't asked her to dance or considered sitting with her. And she was too tired to follow him. Instead, her face dropped into her hands, and she sat alone at the table, her eyes trained on the dancers and her heart heavy.

Chapter Twenty-One

Maree had eaten her fill of the delicious roast beef, potatoes, and vegetables. She'd managed a slice of cheesecake before she was full to the brim and felt happily stuffed. She leaned back in her chair with a smile on her face. It'd been a while since she'd had such a lovely meal, and she'd savoured every bite.

"Would you like to dance?" Jack asked, holding out a hand.

She nodded, took his hand and followed him to the dance floor. How long had it been since a man had held her in his arms? Had led her around the dance floor? She'd been asked out by a few men since Jack left —nothing serious and she'd turned them all down. It was too complicated. But this was different. This was Jack.

The warmth of his arms felt safe and familiar. She leaned in close, swaying in time with his movements as his hand moved up her back. The music was slow and romantic, the lighting dim. He smelled of aftershave and roast beef.

"Why did you come back, Jack?"

He leaned closer to hear over the loud music and chattering guests. "Hmmm?"

"Why did you come back to Sunshine?"

"I already told you…"

"No, I don't mean that line you use. I'm asking what was the real reason you came back."

He met her gaze. "That's hard to answer."

"Try," she said.

He hesitated. "I wanted to see you again."

"You could've seen me anytime over the past five years." Her throat tightened. Emotions were about to pour out, and she fought to control them.

"I know, and I'm sorry. At first, I was in too much grief to think about anyone or anything. Then, when the clouds cleared, I was ashamed. I didn't deserve a second chance, or that's what I thought. I decided that the only way forward was to move on, make a new life for myself. And that's what I did. But it was empty. I couldn't live that way anymore. I missed you."

It was too much. She couldn't take this in. What he was saying … she'd wanted to hear it for so long. But then her heart had closed. She'd had to let him go. It'd been too painful.

She pushed away from him. "I can't…"

And she ran from the dance floor.

She found herself outside on the back patio, gasping for breath. Leaning over the patio railing, she thought back over the past five years, and the ache in her heart grew. Her vision blurred, and she remembered all of Sam's milestones—his birth, first words, first steps, first birthday. Jack had missed it all. She'd longed for him to be part of their lives, and now he wanted that. Could she let him in?

Chapter Twenty-Two

Gwen's date for the wedding was her contractor, Mark. She'd felt awkward inviting him. She hadn't asked a man on a date in ... well, she'd never asked a man on a date in her life. But as soon as they arrived at the reception, she'd forgotten all her awkwardness. He'd immediately suggested dancing, and they'd had an enormous amount of fun bopping and swaying to every tune, fast or slow, until dinner was served. Then, at dinner, he'd chatted amicably with everyone else at the table and had half of them in stitches by the time the main course arrived.

She was a little stunned by how social and outgoing he was. So different to the taciturn Duncan, who usually wanted to leave her events early because he had work to do. Mark was lighthearted, fun, and smiled his way through the evening. It was a pleasure to spend time with him. And after a marriage to a man who most people found a little off-putting, she was grateful to be with someone others liked. It was like a huge green flag, and she felt very happy.

"You know, I was thinking. It might be nice to have

Christmas Eve together," Mark said. "The event at the McLintock Stables finishes early. We could catch up afterwards."

Gwen beamed. "I was thinking the same thing. My plans have changed, since my son Brandon decided to spend Christmas Eve with me and Christmas Day with his wife's family. And so I'm having them over for dinner. Would you like to come?"

"I would love to," he replied, leaning forward to reach for her hand. His touch made her skin tingle. "What should I bring?"

"No need to bring anything. I'll have it all under control."

"I should bring something," he objected.

"You can bring a bottle of wine. That would be lovely."

"Wonderful. I'll pick something out of my cellar."

"You have a wine cellar?"

He laughed. "Remind me to give you a tour of my house."

"I'm looking forward to it."

"I'll be hosting a dinner for a few friends at New Year's. I'd love you to come as my date."

"That sounds like fun. Count me in."

Mark went to the bar and came back with two glasses of port. He handed one to Gwen. "Would you like to get some fresh air?"

She smiled. "I would."

He held out his arm for her to hold, and the two of them strolled out onto the back deck. Twinkle lights sparkled around the outside of the deck and in the branches of the trees surrounding the inn. People were dotted about on chairs, or leaning against the railing, drinking and talking together. The bride and groom had left for their honeymoon, and so the party was slightly more subdued than it had been.

"It was such a nice wedding," she said as she took a seat across from him at a small round table.

"They seem good together."

"They're great together. Emily is really the most gentle, sweet soul. She's become a good friend over the years. And Aaron is a wonderful grandson to Joanna. He's a lovely man."

Just then, Joanna and Chris came outside with glasses of port as well.

"There you are," Joanna said. "We were looking for you. Thought maybe you'd gone back to the dance floor."

"We wanted to get a little bit of air," Gwen replied.

Joanna sat with a sigh. "I'm exhausted. I haven't danced like that in decades."

"It was a great party," Chris said.

"I can't believe he's married. I feel very old." Joanna laughed.

"It goes by in a flash," Gwen said. "My grandkids are still small, but it won't be long, and they'll be doing the same thing. At least, I hope they will. It's such a blessing to live to see your grandchildren grown and happy."

Joanna's eyes glistened at her words. "Amen to that." She raised her glass and clinked it against Gwen's. "And for him to choose my sweet friend, Emily." Her voice broke. "I couldn't have asked for anything more."

"You two are gonna make me cry," Mark grunted as he feigned wiping tears from his eyes. "Let's talk about sports or something."

They all laughed.

Gwen patted his hand. "You always make me smile."

"I try," he said with a wink. "Now, who wants cake?"

Chapter Twenty-Three

The next day, Maree and Sam spent the morning at the beach. She was tired after the wedding. Sam had slept well and was full of energy. He held her hand as he jumped waves for over an hour, and then spent the next hour digging a hole in the sand and building a castle while she lay beside him on her towel, reading a book.

It was nice to have a day off, and she liked to take advantage of every chance she had to spend time with her son. She worked and studied a lot during the week. Sundays were their special day together, just the two of them. She wished she could bottle those days and keep them always with her. The memories of those times were so precious. She'd hold on to them when she was midway through a shift and wanted to get home. Or studying when she felt like she couldn't possibly read another page. The thought of bettering their lives so they could have more days like this together kept her going.

"Mummy, where is Jack?"

Sam's question sent her heart into her throat. Why was he asking about Jack? He hadn't spent much time with him yet, but already Jack's presence was having a big impact on their lives.

"I think he's visiting his family for lunch. Why do you ask?"

"Isn't it my family too?"

She sat up on her towel and put down the book. "Uh … yes, that's right. Your family too. Our family, I guess."

"Can I meet them?"

She'd been expecting this question would come up sometime, but not so soon. She wasn't ready for it yet, and the pain of his words hit her like a mallet. She hadn't realised just how much bitterness she'd held against Jack's family for abandoning her when he did. How much she'd held it against them that they weren't there for her, to help her, to reach out, to meet Sam. She'd cut them off after they failed to support her when Jack left. Although she knew it was more complicated than that—they'd lost a son, and they were grieving. Still, she couldn't help blaming them for what'd happened. Why didn't they talk to Jack? Intervene? Do something?

"Yes, you can meet them," she said, measuring her words carefully.

"What's wrong, Mummy? Don't you like them?"

"I like them a lot. They're very nice people."

"So, why don't they want to see us?"

"I'm sure they will. The thing is, honey, they didn't know about you. I haven't spoken to them in a long time, and they didn't realise you were born. It's complicated…"

She didn't know what else to say. How could she tell him what'd happened? As she spoke the words, they sounded hollow, meaningless. She should've tried harder. Done more. It wasn't fair to Sam. They were his family. Guilt made her throat ache.

"That's okay. I'll see them soon."

She wanted to hug him with relief. "Yes, you'll see them

soon, I'm sure. I don't know when, but we'll talk about it. Okay?"

"Okay."

"Did you remember that Grandma and Grandpa are coming to visit this afternoon? They're meeting us in the park in a few minutes. We'll have to pack up and head that way shortly."

"Oh, yeah, okay. Let me finish this sandcastle."

Her parents had flown in that morning and were currently driving to Sunshine in a rental. They'd changed plans suddenly to come and visit her and Sam before the holidays. She was looking forward to seeing them, although she'd have to take a deep breath and prepare for the judgement. They always had a lot of opinions about her life when they flew in and out of it.

A few minutes later, she and Sam had packed up his toys and the towels, and they trudged up the beach to wash under the shower. His face was pink, though she'd put plenty of sunscreen on him earlier. But they'd been in the sun for hours, and it would be good to get a break under the shade of the sails that covered the BBQ area by the playground.

After he was dried off and dressed, Maree tied a sarong around her bikini and set up a folding chair in the shade while Sam played on the playground with some other children around his age. Within a few minutes, her parents arrived.

She embraced her father and then her mother. They both looked so much older than the last time she'd seen them, and it took her breath away for a moment. She should make an effort to call them more often.

"How are you?" she asked as they set up chairs beside her.

"My hip is playing up, but otherwise I'm well," Mum said.

Her father grunted. "The country is going to the dogs, but I suppose we'll survive it."

She smiled. "Glad to see nothing much has changed."

He grinned. "You know I'm too old to change."

Sam came running over then to greet them. He sat on her mother's lap and told her all about his day. She gave him a gift, a book that he unwrapped quickly and then handed to Maree to put in her bag. Then he was off again, back to the playground to slide and swing.

"He's growing up," Dad said, leaning back in his chair.

"So big now," Mum agreed, wiping her eyes.

"You should visit more often," Maree said. "It goes by quickly."

The two of them exchanged a look.

"Yes, we should," Mum said.

Maree had expected them to fight, push back, say they were too busy. But they didn't. She wasn't sure what to say.

"I need to talk to the two of you about Jack."

Dad's nostrils flared. "What about him?"

"I know you have opinions about him..."

"He left you and Sam all alone," Mum snapped. "He deserves every bit of our anger."

"He didn't know about Sam."

"But he knew about you. Oh, I want to give him a piece of my mind."

"Okay, Mum. Hold that thought, because he's back in town."

They both gaped at her in silence.

She nodded. "Yep, he's back in Sunshine and has moved in across the hall from our flat. And before you say anything else, yes, he's met Sam and knows he's Sam's father. I told him recently, and he's been really great about it. He forgives me for not telling him, he says he regrets leaving me, and he's asked for regular visitation with Sam going forward."

Mum sighed. "He's back."

"Yep."

"And I'm sure you're just letting him walk all over you again, like you always do."

Maree bit her tongue.

Dad stared at the ground. "What does Sam think?"

"He's excited about finally knowing his dad. He doesn't say much. But he likes spending time with him."

"It's about time," Dad said. "A boy needs to know his father."

"You should've dealt with this years ago," Mum added, anger making her voice sound cold.

"I know, Mum. You're right. I should've. But I didn't. I can't change the past; I can only work on the present."

"Well, I suppose we don't have much say in any of it."

"Not really—I'm just letting you know that Sam and Jack are going to have a relationship. As of right now, I don't know how that will look. But I'd like the two of you to get on board and forgive Jack for the past. He's apologised to me several times now and says it's the biggest regret of his life. I'd like us to give him some grace. He is Sam's father."

Mum scowled. "I don't know..."

"Oh, give it up, Jean. Give the boy a break. He made a mistake. We all do that sometimes."

Maree couldn't help smiling at the way her father still called Jack a boy. In his mind, Jack would always be the teenager who climbed into her bedroom window and got caught in the fly screen.

Chapter Twenty-Four

The sound of carols rose into the air around Maree. She sat on a picnic rug next to Sam, who was happily munching on a fried chicken leg. He wore a crown of glow sticks in red and yellow. On a stage at the front of the green, a choir sang, their voices high and clear through the sound system. Jemma and Dan were perched on folding chairs behind them.

"Would you like some potato salad?" Jemma asked as she passed Maree the dish.

Maree took it and scooped some onto her own plate and then Sam's. "Delicious. Thank you. This is amazing."

"Your chicken is the best," Jemma replied. "Isn't it, Dan?"

Dan nodded, chewing. He swallowed. "Love it. And this salad is great too, if I may say so."

"You did a great job on it," Jemma said with a laugh as she patted his leg.

Gwen and Mark sat on folding chairs behind the picnic rugs. Gwen wore a pair of jeans and a red shirt with a gold chain necklace. Lately, she'd been dressing more glamorously than usual and carried herself with a new air of confidence. Maree had noticed it at work, but it followed her wherever she went now. She wondered if it was being the owner of a successful boutique inn, or maybe it was the budding relationship with her contractor. Whatever it was, it suited her.

With a smile, Maree turned back to listen to Sam, who was tugging on her sleeve.

"Mum, is Santa coming? When is Santa coming?"

She smiled and tapped the end of his nose gently with her fingertip. "Santa is coming very soon. I don't think they'll make you wait much longer. Just be patient and eat your dinner."

The voices of the crowd around them swelled to join with the singers on stage as everyone sang a well-known carol. Maree loved this time of year. It felt good to be part of a community that came together to celebrate Christmas as one. No one worried about the person next to them belting out an off-pitch tune. They all sang in unison, with loud voices, enjoying the moment of togetherness.

"Daddy!" Sam's voice reverberated loudly above the noise of the crowd.

Maree's heart skipped a beat. *Daddy.* It was the first time he'd used that word. She searched the green and spotted Jack weaving his way through the picnic blankets and folding chairs in the gathering dusk. He wore a pair of shorts, a white T-shirt, and a cap on his head. Caps suited him. She'd always liked them on him. They made him look even more sporty than usual. That plus the T-shirt, which showed off his toned arms.

He joined them on the picnic rug, throwing himself down beside Sam with a laugh. "Hey, mate."

Sam jumped up and down in place. "I knew you'd come. Did you bring me anything?"

"Sam, that's not polite," Maree said, feeling flustered.

"No, it's okay. He's right—I did bring him something." Jack reached into a pocket and pulled out a bag of marshmallows. "I don't know if you like marshmallows, but I'm a big fan..."

"I love them!" Sam shouted. He reached for the treats with a grin, but Jack pulled the bag away.

"I'm sure your mum wants you to finish dinner first, right?" he asked, giving Maree a quick glance.

She nodded. "Yes, please. Clean that plate and you can have a marshmallow."

As Sam continued to work on his dinner, Jack scooted closer to Maree on the rug until his fingers lightly touched hers. He sat with his hands behind him, his knees bent before him. Maree had her hands behind her with her legs crossed. Her heart rate accelerated.

"I didn't realise you were coming," she said.

"I'm here with my family. My parents." He nodded his head to the left.

Maree looked where he indicated and saw his parents and sister seated over on the edge of the crowd. At this distance, she couldn't see the expression on their faces, but they seemed to be intently studying the stage rather than looking in her direction. Did they want to see her again? Did they want to get to know Sam? She couldn't figure them out. She'd thought she was one of them for such a long time, that they loved her and accepted her as part of their family. But then, they'd abandoned her almost as readily as Jack had. She wasn't sure how she could look beyond that. But she'd try, for Sam's sake.

"How are they?" she said, swallowing around the bitterness in her throat.

"They're fine. They want to see you." He searched her face for a reaction.

She offered him a wan smile. "Oh?"

"They'd love to meet Sam."

"That's good. I want them to know him. Only ... they

didn't seem interested in staying in touch. I know I should be able to put that behind me."

He shrugged. "You should feel however you choose to. You have a right. My parents are so ashamed of how they behaved. They told me they thought you must've done something to drive me away. They blamed you for a while, but only because they were in so much grief over losing my brother, and then losing contact with me. They weren't thinking clearly. I hope you can see that."

"I suppose that makes sense, although it doesn't make it any easier on me. I've been on my own for so long. My own parents only make flying visits. They've already gone back to their travels after a quick stopover in Sunshine. I won't see them again for months. So, I've been raising Sam by myself," she whispered in an attempt to keep it from Sam. She didn't like badmouthing anyone, let alone family, in front of him. She didn't want him to hear about her struggles in raising him.

Thankfully, he paid her no attention, rooting around in the marshmallow bag and pulling them out one by one to gleefully shove into his mouth.

"I know you have, and we're all sorry about that. Words won't help—I get it. But if we'd known..."

"You couldn't know."

"We could go around and around in this spiral of guilt, shame, and apologising—me, then you, then my parents, then me again ... but I don't know how much can be gained from it."

"You're right. I'm sick of the whole thing, to be honest."

"I'd like to start fresh. My family would too."

"I'd love that as well," she said, relieved. "It's just what I need. Some spiked eggnog and a fresh start." She laughed.

"Now that, I can do. I'll be right back." He got to his feet and jogged over to his parents, then soon returned with a large thermos and two glasses. "Freshly made spiked eggnog." He waggled his eyebrows. "You know Mum makes the best in town."

Marie laughed. "I was only joking. But I won't say no." Jack poured the eggnog and handed her the glass. She took a sip. "You're right. It's as delicious as I remember."

Just then, a soloist took the stage. It was Debbie Holmes. She wore a long red dress that shimmered under the spotlight. Her hair was perfectly groomed into a grey bob, and she looked extra tall in her spiky red heels.

"Look, it's Debbie," Maree cried.

Debbie opened her mouth, and a beautiful deep voice reverberated across the crowd, making everyone hush. She sang "Silent Night" so beautifully, it brought tears to Maree's eyes.

"I had no idea Debbie could sing like that," Jemma said, wiping her eyes as Debbie left the stage and joined her husband in an embrace.

"Wow," Maree agreed. "That was so good. I wish I could sing. It's such a talent."

"She was great. But you have a good voice too. You used to sing all the time."

"I was horrible," Maree objected, laughing.

"You were cute."

"Fine, I was cute but horrible."

"Okay, I can admit it, your pitch was a little off. But I gave you an A for effort." Jack grinned at her.

She leaned against his shoulder, wishing everything could be different. That they'd never been apart. That they lived in a marriage that was as strong and passionate as it used to be. That they weren't divorced.

Her heart lurched at the memory of that day when the divorce papers arrived. She'd been stricken by the pain of it, the baby in her belly showing. How could he leave her? Walk away after everything they'd had together?

But it was time for a new start. To put that behind her. Not to forget, but to stop reminding herself. Give him a chance to make it up to them. Everyone deserved a second chance, and she and Sam could give that to Jack. It was the least she could do for the father of her child. Even if he walked away again, she could say that she'd let him get to know his son.

"Let's go and see your family," she said, getting to her feet.

"Are you sure you're ready?"

"I'm ready. Come on, Sam. We're going to see your grandparents."

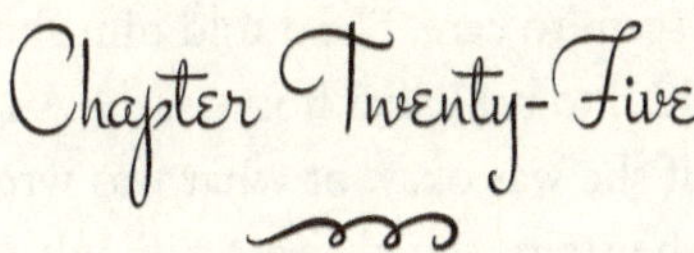

Chapter Twenty-Five

After Carols by Candlelight, Jemma wasn't feeling well, so Dan took her home. They didn't stay for dessert with Maree, Jack, and Sam. There was a food truck serving churros with chocolate sauce and ice cream, which looked and smelled delicious. But she'd suddenly felt nauseated, and there was a pain in her abdomen that wouldn't go away.

Dan leaped up the stairs ahead of her and rushed into the unit. She thought he was going ahead to help her, but instead he threw on the television and plonked down into the armchair to turn on the tennis.

"We're just in time to see the end of the game," he said, rubbing his hands together.

Jemma glared at him through narrowed eyes. "Really?"

"Yep."

He didn't hear the sarcasm in her voice. Didn't even look up.

"I guess I'll just get myself a glass of water and go to bed."

He waved over his head. "Okay. Goodnight, honey."

Jemma stood in the kitchen to drink a glass of cold water. It soothed her parched throat and made her stomach churn at the same time. She leaned against the counter and breathed through a wave of pain. That couldn't be good. Anxiety kick-started in her chest.

What if she lost the baby?

Dan didn't seem to care. She'd told him she wasn't feeling well, had asked him to bring her home early. And yet he hadn't asked her once if she was okay, or what was wrong. He hadn't helped her up the stairs, which were difficult to climb in the state she was in. Instead, he was fixated on watching sports.

If she said anything, he'd jump up to help her and declare he couldn't read her mind. She'd heard it all before. But sometimes, she wanted him to *know* that something was wrong. As her husband, shouldn't he have some kind of insight into what was going on with his wife? If he loved her, wouldn't he be in tune with how she was feeling? Especially since she was carrying their child inside her body.

After she'd drained the glass, she padded to the bedroom, climbed into her pjs and into bed. But before she could close her eyes, pain stabbed through her gut. She cried out and clutched at her rounded belly.

"What is happening?" she whispered, squeezing her eyes shut. "Please don't let me lose the baby."

"Did you say something?" Dan came into the room. When he saw her, his eyes widened. "What's wrong?"

"I don't know. I'm in a lot of pain." She sat up, swinging her feet to the floor, then doubling over again. "Oh, it hurts."

"Should we go to the hospital?"

"I think we have to," she said, standing to her feet and immediately falling back onto the bed with another groan. Tears sprang to her eyes. "I don't want to lose another baby."

"Don't jump to conclusions. We don't know what's happening yet. I'll get the keys. Is there anything you need?"

"My shoes and purse."

"Wait there." He hurried and found her socks and

sneakers and bent to put them on her feet. He found her purse in the closet and slung it over her shoulder. "Let's go."

He helped her to the car and strapped her in, and then hurried around to the driver's side. She leaned her head back and shut her eyes to pray. This couldn't be happening. Not now. She was in the second trimester. Her miscarriages had all occurred before twelve weeks. This was too late. Tears welled in her eyes, and she couldn't fight them any longer.

Dan started the car and glanced at her. "It's going to be okay, honey. Don't worry about anything yet. We've got to stay positive."

She nodded, sniffling back her tears. "Okay."

Positive. She could do that. She inhaled a long, slow breath.

The hospital wasn't very busy, and it didn't take long for a doctor to see them. They put her in a wheelchair and wheeled her through to get an ultrasound. When the technician showed them both the heartbeat on the screen, she breathed an audible sigh of relief.

"The baby's okay?"

"The heartbeat looks strong. I'll get the doctor for you. She can explain what's going on."

Jemma cleaned the gel from her stomach and got dressed while they waited. Dan paced the floor of the room. In a matter of minutes, the doctor knocked and came into the room. She sat on a stool and smiled at them.

"I know you've had a bit of a scare, but everything looks good. The baby is healthy. The heartbeat is strong. I think what you've experienced are some Braxton Hicks contractions."

"Is that bad?" Dan asked.

The doctor shook her head. "It's a little early, but it's fine. You're doing great. Nothing to worry about. Try to relax. Sometimes anxiety can cause more aches and pains during pregnancy, so do your best to find ways to be peaceful and happy."

Jemma nodded and thanked the doctor, then sat on the hard chair and stared at the floor. How could she be peaceful with the way Dan had been acting? Of course she was anxious. She wasn't sure what she was going to do about her workaholic husband, the man who'd said all he wanted was to have a family with her and then showed no signs of wanting that baby when she became pregnant.

He lay a hand on her back. "You ready?"

She nodded. "Let's go home."

Chapter Twenty-Six

One of the things that Maree tried not to do, as a single mother, was to rack up debt on her credit card. She'd applied for it a few years ago for the points. She wanted to travel one day, and what better way to make it happen than with frequent flyer points? But now she stared at that card and then at the bicycle on the store shelf in front of her, and back again.

Would it be bad to put a few things on the credit card that she couldn't afford to repay? It would only be for a few months. She was sure she could pay it back within three instalments. Maybe five or six, at most. Although, with interest, that might draw the payments out a little longer.

What was she thinking? Sam didn't need a bike. Not that badly. But he did want one. Oh, this was too hard. She longed to give him the Christmas he wanted, but she'd already used up their allotted money for the month. When she got her next paycheck, Christmas would be over, and she wouldn't be able to afford to buy the entire bike then anyway. Maybe she could do a payment plan, but it wouldn't be a Christmas present if it was still in the shop on Christmas morning.

She sighed and walked along the aisle, eying each of the

bikes to see if any of them would be better. She could get the cheaper one and find the most affordable helmet. That was the best she could manage, although maybe she should look for a garage sale or online to see if she could find something secondhand.

"Christmas shopping?" Jack's voice startled her.

She spun around to see him walking down the aisle toward her.

"How did you guess?" She flashed him a smile.

He stopped and crossed his arms, looking at the bikes.

"Is he ready for training wheels?"

She nodded. "He's dying to learn. And even though we live in a unit, I told him we could try riding in the parking lot. I don't think anyone would mind."

"Sounds like a good plan. Which bike are you thinking?"

She sighed. "I don't know. They're all pretty expensive, but that blue one looks like him. Don't you think?" She pointed at the bike.

"I like it. Or that black one."

She laughed. "Trust you to go for the most expensive bike in the store."

"I have expensive taste. I can't help it."

"Well, I can't afford that one. Or any of them, really. But I'm going to figure something out."

"Let me know if I can do anything."

"Thanks, I appreciate it. But I want to do this for him. He's been asking for this thing for so long. And I've been hoping to save up the money, but it's hard with the day-to-day."

"I can understand that. I'll tell you what—why don't we grab some lunch together, my treat. And we can talk about Christmas plans, and anything else you'd like to discuss."

She smiled. "That sounds nice. I could use a break. Sam's at daycare today, and I'm supposed to be studying, but I thought I should try to get some Christmas shopping done while he's not with me. And I needed to get away from the books for a while."

"I'll buy you some food, and we'll forget all about books, kids, and Christmas gifts for half an hour."

She laughed. "Perfect."

They found a booth in the back of a small Thai restaurant, and Maree slid in one side with Jack in the other. They ordered and then sipped green tea while they waited for their food to arrive.

"This brings back memories," Jack said.

Maree looked around. "Have we been here?"

"Not this place in particular. But we used to love going out for Thai."

"True. It's my favourite takeaway."

"Mine too." His gaze fixed on hers, making her breath catch. His grey eyes were so full of intensity, they drew her in.

"I thought it might be nice if you came over on Christmas morning. You could watch Sam open his gifts, if you like. Jemma and Dan won't be there, since they'll probably sleep late and then they have brunch plans. So, it'll only be us. Of course, if you're busy..."

"I'm not busy. And I'd love to join you."

"Great." She grinned. "Sam will be so happy. Fair warning, it will be early."

"Early is fine with me. After last night, when you and Sam left, Mum asked if you would like to come over for lunch on Christmas Eve. I totally understand if that's too much, but my whole family will be there, and they really want you and Sam there too."

Maree swallowed a mouthful of tea. It was what she'd wanted for so long. But now she felt like an intruder. An outsider, looking in. "I don't know..."

"I get it—it's too soon. Too much. But think about it, okay?"

"It's just that ... with your family, I feel a bit like I'm not welcome. And maybe that's my insecurity after everything that happened."

"You're definitely welcome."

"I know we're not supposed to do apologies any longer—we've done too many. And I'm not asking for that. But do you think they really want me there? Or are they only trying to make you happy?"

"They definitely want you there. They were so excited that you agreed to see them last night. They were scared you'd never talk to them again."

She sighed. "I don't hold a grudge..."

"I know you don't. It's one of the many things I love about you. But this time you have every right to hold a grudge. I hope you won't."

"I won't, I promise." She drew a deep breath. "Okay, I'll come to Christmas-Eve lunch. And I'll try to be confident and not think about being an outsider. It'll be fine. I'm sure of it."

"Great. Mum will be so happy. I'll call her when we're finished lunch."

Their food arrived. Green chicken curry and beef massaman with coconut rice and coconut prawns. It smelled delectable as Maree piled spoonfuls of each dish onto her plate.

Jack took a bite, then swallowed a mouthful of Thai beer. "There's something else I want to talk to you about as well."

She nodded, chewing happily.

"As you know, I haven't had the chance to contribute towards Sam's childhood so far. And I'd really like to do that."

"I'd like that too. How do you see that looking?" She sipped her wine.

"Financially, I'd like to give you child support payments. I don't really even know how that works, but I'll look into it. And we'll figure it out."

"Really?" She hadn't ever planned to ask for help. She liked to be independent, to do it on her own. She liked to be able to say that she didn't need anyone else. But lately, things had been even tougher than usual, and she often found herself running out of steam and wondering if they'd be able to make the rent.

"Would that help?"

"It would help a lot," she replied. "I'm struggling a bit because I'm trying to study so I can get a better-paying job in the future. But in the meantime, I'm only able to work part time at the inn, which isn't really enough for us to live on. So, anything you can contribute would help."

"I'm so happy you're okay with this. It would mean a lot to me to be able to help out with Sam."

"That would be nice," she said. "He'd like that."

He reached across the table and took her hand, squeezing it gently. "I can't tell you how much you and Sam mean to me. And I'm so grateful you're willing to let me back into your life. I promise, I won't let you down again."

She met his gaze. "I hope that's true, Jack. Because Sam deserves a father who'll stick around."

He raised her hand to his lips and kissed the back of it. "I'm not going anywhere. I won't leave the two of you ever again. I promise you that. Do you believe me?"

She sighed. "I want to, Jack..."

"That's good enough for now. I'll prove it to you."

She withdrew her hand. "I'm glad you're back in our lives. I'll try to trust you again."

"It's up to me to rebuild that trust, and I'm going to do that."

She watched him as he ate and chatted about his business. She nodded every now and then, joining in with comments and exclamations. But all she could think about was how much she wanted to be in his arms with him reassuring her that everything was going to be okay. That he was in their lives forever, and he'd never leave. He'd said the words, but could she trust him? She wanted to. And she'd try. But it would take time to restore what was broken.

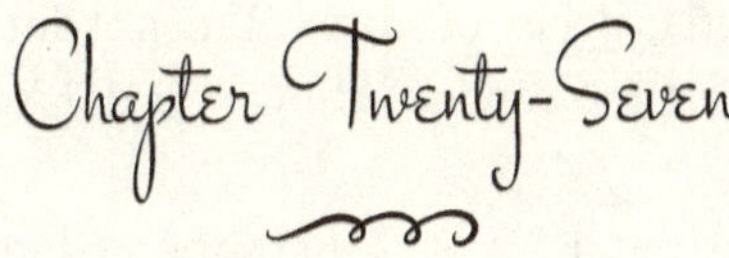

Chapter Twenty-Seven

The television flickered with a sports match of some kind, but Jemma couldn't be bothered to look at it. Instead, her attention was on the Christmas tree. The poor little tree with hardly a gift beneath it for Sam or Maree. She'd have to do something to help her friend, but Maree was proud. She didn't like to accept help.

"We should get Sam something for Christmas," she said.

Dan grunted but didn't look away from the screen. He sat with his legs spread out on the couch so that his toes were touching Jemma's thigh.

"Did you hear me?"

His head swivelled. "Huh?"

"We should buy something for Sam. Look at the tree—there's hardly anything beneath it."

"I'm sure Maree's going to stuff it with gifts on Christmas Eve. Santa hasn't come yet." He smiled. "You worry too much. The doctor told you to stay calm."

"I'm calm," she huffed. "I just worry that..."

"You're worrying. See? I knew you were. You can't get worried. It's not up to us. You know how Maree is. She won't thank you for interfering in her Christmas plans for Sam. Let her handle it. I'm sure she has it all under control. You'll see—tomorrow night, the tree will be jam-packed with gifts. I guarantee it."

She straightened her posture. "I'm not interfering. And I'm not worrying too much. I think you don't worry *enough* about things."

His eyes narrowed. "What's that supposed to mean?"

She'd had it. She'd been quiet for far too long. It was time they hashed things out. She had to know where he stood.

"Do you want this baby?"

He sat up, letting his feet fall to the floor. "What? Of course I do."

"Because it doesn't seem like it."

He turned to face her. "How can you say that? I've been killing myself..."

"You've been everywhere but here."

"I have to work, Jemma! You know that. You're leaving me in the lurch."

"I'm not leaving you in the lurch. I'm having a baby. A baby that we both wanted. This is our family. I'm doing this for us." Tears filled her eyes and clogged her throat.

He reached for her hand. "Why are we fighting? I don't understand."

His soft tone melted her anger away. "I don't feel like you want this baby. You've been gone since I told you about the pregnancy. And you haven't taken a single moment to celebrate with me. You seem angry, not happy."

He sighed. "I'm so happy. Did I forget to say that?"

"You completely forgot." She sniffled.

He pulled her to him and wrapped an arm around her shoulders while he kissed the top of her head softly. "I'm over the moon that you're finally pregnant. I guess I got caught up in making sure the business continues thriving. You've done so much work to get us to where we are..."

"We both have," she corrected him.

"Yes, we've done the work together. But I don't want to let you down. I don't want to lose the momentum you've built. And I want to make sure I'm taking care of you and the baby. Plus trying for so long, I think it wore both of us down. Now that you're pregnant, I feel the pressure of it. It's a lot to manage on my own."

"But you're not alone."

"I know that. I shouldn't have acted as though I was. I get stressed."

"I'm worried about things too, but we can't turn on each other. I need you to be happy about the baby. To spend time with me. To enjoy this season of life together." Her heart hurt as the words poured out of her. She'd felt so alone and her throat swelled with unshed tears.

"But I have so much work to do."

"I understand that, and I'll support you in it. But you need to take time for me and the baby as well. Our lives are only going to get busier. And I don't want to feel as though I'm a single mother, doing this all on my own. You've really hurt me lately, with your attitude."

He sighed. "I'm sorry, baby. I didn't mean to do that. I guess I've felt a distance between us for a long time now. The miscarriages and wanting to get pregnant — all of that took over. We haven't really spent time together, just having fun, in so long."

Her heart ached at his words. "I know what you mean. I've felt it too."

"I want things to be different. I guess I don't know how to make that happen."

She reached for his hand. "We'll get through this together. I need you and you need me. That's why we make such a great team. No one is the hero. We're both important—in each other's lives but also for this baby. He or she is going to need both of us. But I don't want to spend this happy time worrying about what might go wrong or how to pay the bills. Those things will work themselves out. All I want is for us to be happy, to celebrate together because this pregnancy is a miracle. We didn't know if we were ever going to get here. Let's not rush this moment by panicking over real estate or bills."

"You're absolutely right. We should celebrate. What would you like to do?"

She nestled into his chest. "I want to stay right here."

"That's it? You don't want some non-alcoholic champagne? Maybe a night out on the town? We could go dancing. It's still early." He kissed her forehead.

She frowned. "I'd go for some hot chocolate and a fruit-mince pie. But otherwise, I'd like to stay right here." She snuggled in even closer. "This is my favourite place in the whole world. I feel deliriously happy and safe here. I could live here."

He laughed. "I'll get you the hot chocolate and fruit-mince pie and be right back. Do you want to watch a Christmas movie?"

"But you're watching the..." She peered at the screen. "Tennis..."

"I don't mind. As long as you're okay and I'm with you, I'm good."

"A Christmas movie sounds great. How about *The Santa Clause*?"

He nodded. "Coming right up."

After he left to get her drink and snack in the kitchen, she made herself comfortable on the couch. With one hand cupping her swollen belly, she smiled through a veil of happy tears.

"It's all going to be okay, little one. Your daddy loves you, and so does your mummy. And we're going to have such a good life together. We can't wait for you to get here."

Dan soon returned with two mugs of steaming hot chocolate and set them down on the coffee table.

"I added cinnamon and marshmallows to make them a bit more Christmas-y."

"Mmm ... perfect." She took a sip. "Delicious. Thanks."

"And I brought the whole pack of pies because it's impossible to stop at one."

She laughed. "You know me so well. Hand it over, Mr. Grant."

He gave her the pack of pies, and she pulled one out. "I'm going to make crumbs."

He jumped up again and raced back to the kitchen, calling over his shoulder, "Two plates on their way."

When they were both finally snug on the couch again, he found the movie she wanted, and they settled down to watch together. This time, he had his arms around her, and she was nestled against his chest, feeling satisfied and full of joy. This was everything she was hoping for.

She'd completely misunderstood her husband's reaction to the pregnancy announcement. He'd always been the conscientious type and had grown up with parents who didn't show him much affection. Instead, they displayed their love by doing things for him—paying for him to attend university, helping him buy a car, washing his clothes and bringing him groceries whenever they popped by to visit. She'd never seen them embrace him or tell him they loved him, but they showed it with their actions.

It'd been hard for him in childhood to feel their love through their actions without any kind of words to back it up, but he'd realised in adulthood that they'd simply developed a different way of loving. And even though it forced a kind of distance between them, Jemma could see that their family had a lot of respect for one another. She'd done her best to fit in with them, to understand them, to see their acts of service as an act of love.

But she'd forgotten that their son might behave in much the same way under pressure. She would have to remind herself to give him grace in the future and to talk to him about how she was feeling. She looked up at his handsome face, his eyes already drooping shut, and felt blessed. He was a good man and a good husband. One day soon, he'd make a great father. She could finally relax and enjoy the fact that they were building their family after such a long wait. And it felt good.

Chapter Twenty-Eight

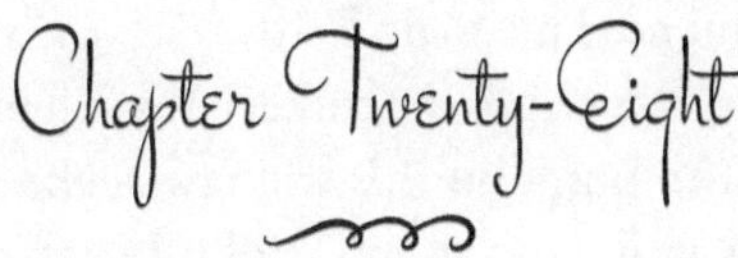

Gwen was flustered. The rest of the family were all elsewhere for the evening, so she'd invited Brandon's family over for Christmas Eve dinner. And her turkey wasn't cooked yet, the potato bake was still crunchy, and the salad looked a bit limp. When Mark knocked at the door, she wasn't dressed for dinner and hadn't done her hair yet.

She glanced at her reflection in the mirror by the front door and saw a smudge of flour on one cheek, some in her hair making it even more grey than usual, and a big stain on the front of her apron. Too late to do anything about that now. She pulled the door open with a smile.

"Hello! Thanks for coming early. I could really use some help. I'm a little concerned about the timing…"

He stepped through the doorway and handed her a bottle of red wine. "I'm sure it's going to be wonderful. And I hope you like the wine."

"Thank you so much. Come on in."

She shut the door behind him. He looked so handsome in his blue buttoned shirt and khaki slacks. His hair was combed back so that it was a little spiky, and he smelled of aftershave in a way that made her knees weak.

He kissed her on the cheek then clapped his hands together. "Okay, just point me in the right direction, and I'll do whatever you need me to do."

"Can you please watch the turkey? It's still in the oven and I don't want it to burn, but it's still raw at the moment. The potato bake as well. And if you could decant the wine, that would be great. I'm going to take a shower, if that's okay?"

He smiled. "I've got it all under control."

She hurried to her bedroom and quickly took a shower. She brushed the flour out of her hair—no time to wash and style it. She'd simply have to add some curls, and that would have to suffice. After she'd added makeup and stepped into her purple dress, she was finally pleased with the reflection staring back at her from the bathroom mirror.

"Much better."

She hurried out to the table and found that Mark had finished setting it. There was soft Christmas music playing, the scent of roast turkey filled the air, and Mark stood over a pot, stirring, with her apron wrapped around his waist.

She watched him for a moment, moving in time to the music as he stirred, humming along to the tune. It was a precious sight to see, and a lump formed in her throat. How she longed to share her life with someone just like him. It was early in the relationship—they hadn't even shared a kiss yet— but she could see herself building a life with him. In this moment, he filled her apartment with a presence that gave her so much peace and hope for the future.

"This looks wonderful," she said.

He glanced up. "Wow."

She smiled and spun in place. "You like my dress?"

"I like it a lot." He grinned. "You look beautiful."

"Thank you. You look pretty good yourself. And everything is smelling divine, which is a much better situation than it was when I left you alone."

"I haven't done much. But I saw this cranberry sauce recipe sitting open and the ingredients on the bench, so I thought I'd throw it together for you. It's pretty much done."

She peered over his arm into the saucepan. "You're a miracle worker. Thank you."

When she looked up at him, he was staring at her with a half-smile hanging about his lips. His eyes darkened, and the smile faded. She waited, her lips tingling with anticipation. She recognised the look of desire, and it sent a delightful shiver through her.

But at that moment, the doorbell rang, followed by Brandon's entire family charging through the door and into the small unit.

"Merry Christmas!" Brandon shouted, his arms laden with gifts.

He went to the tree and placed the gifts beneath it, then hurried to kiss Gwen's cheek. "How are you, Mum? You look amazing. And this must be the famous Mark."

Mark exchanged an amused look with Gwen. "Famous?"

She shrugged. "I was very appreciative of the work you did at the inn. That must be what he's referring to."

"Of course." Mark laughed. He shook Brandon's hand, and then greeted the rest of the family.

Brandon's wife, Mara, wore a long, flowing dress, and her golden hair fell down her tanned back in natural waves. She embraced Gwen.

"It smells so good in here. We're starving. The kids have been driving us mad all the way over here."

Gwen said hello to each of the kids then sent them to wash up for dinner. Mark helped her set all the food on the table. While they ate, the kids were rowdy. They talked over one another in their excitement about Christmas and the gifts they might receive. Gwen loved every moment of it.

Brandon had four children under twelve years of age. They were growing up so fast. She'd spent a good portion of their childhood caring for them when their parents were at work. She knew them so well and was proud of the caring children they were turning into.

"What do you want for Christmas?" Kimmy asked, her green eyes blinking as she stabbed at a carrot on her plate.

Gwen hesitated. "What I'd really love is for your Aunty Beth to be able to come home. But I know she can't. She's spending Christmas with Damien in Sydney."

"I'm going to miss her," Kimmy said dramatically. "I hope she comes home soon."

"I do too," Gwen replied.

Beside her, Mark offered her a sympathetic smile. "It's hard letting go. I know what it's like. My kids are all married, and they take turns at the other family's house every other Christmas. I've got them tomorrow, but next year I'll have Christmas Eve with them instead. Thankfully, everyone lives fairly close by, so it's not such a big deal."

"That sounds like it works well."

"I think so. At least, so far it does. I don't know what will happen once the grandkids are teenagers. They'll probably have their own ideas about what they want to do then."

"I suppose it will be time for new traditions," Gwen said.

He smiled at her, his blue eyes crinkled at the edges. "Yes, I suppose it will."

Chapter Twenty-Nine

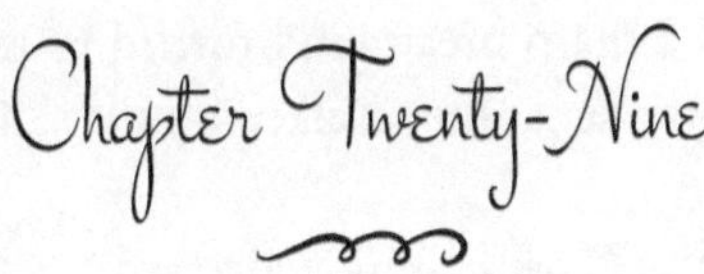

"I'm so glad you're coming over for Christmas Eve lunch," Jack said as he turned the wheel of his truck into his parents' long, curving driveway.

"Me too," Maree said, although her heart skidded in her chest at the sight of the large grey mansion as it rose up against the backdrop of the private golden beach where she'd swam so many times over the years.

"I hope Sam doesn't mind that Santa brought some of his gifts to my parents' house this year." Jack glanced in the rearview mirror.

Maree swivelled to get a look at her son. He'd been so quiet riding in the car seat Jack had bought and strapped into his truck for him. Was he okay? This was a lot for him to deal with. A whole new family, full of people he didn't know.

"Do you think Santa could find it?" Sam asked.

"He's been here before. He definitely knows the way." Jack winked at Maree, making her smile.

They parked in front of the house. Maree climbed out of the truck and strained her neck to look up at the imposing structure. Not exactly suited to the beach landscape. There was so much concrete, and it was adorned with statues and water fountains. Nerves fluttered in her stomach. Would they be happy to see her and Sam here? What would they say?

She inhaled a sharp breath and turned to reach for Sam's hand. He clung to her as they walked up the stairs to the front door.

"Is this a house?" Sam asked, wide-eyed.

Jack laughed. "Yes, it's a house. This is where I grew up."

"It's so big."

"It's very big, I know. But I promise, you're going to love it here. We have our own beach, and we can go down there later to make a sandcastle and take a swim, if you want."

The sun beat down on the back of Maree's neck as she waited at the door while Jack rang the doorbell. Sweat trickled down her temples. She adjusted her grip on the box of biscuits she'd brought for the family.

The massive timber door swung open, and Margaret Houston greeted them with open arms. Her blonde bob didn't move at all as she leaned in to kiss Maree's cheek, and then to hug a sullen Sam, who had one hand still in Maree's.

"Welcome to our home. Merry Christmas. Come inside—it's so hot out here."

They found Jack's father, Tom, and his sister, Meg, in the living room. Everyone was very welcoming to Maree and Sam. Before long, Sam was in the kitchen, helping his grandmother and aunt put the finishing touches on the meal.

Maree sat in the living room with Jack and Tom, glancing worriedly at the kitchen every now and then. Should she go in there and make sure he was okay?

"He's fine—don't worry about him. Mum is probably feeding him candy, but he's otherwise in good hands," Jack assured her.

She drew a deep breath. "You're right. I'm used to having

to watch him constantly. But I'm sure your mother and Meg can manage him and won't let him run with a knife."

Jack laughed but then got to his feet and hurried into the kitchen. She could hear the murmur of voices, then he returned.

"All good. I reminded them about what four-year-olds can get up to."

She smiled. "Thank you. People forget how quick they can be when it comes to grabbing something hot or sharp."

"I'm still getting used to it myself," Jack said.

"And how are you these days?" Tom asked. "We haven't seen you in so long. It's good to catch up."

"I'm fine. I'm studying financial planning and working part time at the Aurora Inn."

"That's right. Gwen has done a wonderful job renovating the place."

"I think so too."

"Financial planning, huh? That's a good area to get into."

"I'm hoping to get a career going so that Sam and I can have a better future."

"I'll bet it's been a struggle over the years. I wish we'd been able to help." Tom cleared his throat.

"I'm sorry…"

"No, let's not get into all that again. I didn't mean anything by it. Let's talk about the future instead. I'm glad to hear you're studying. It's good for young people to aim for something. You've got to have a bit of fire in the belly at your age. Keeps you going."

She smiled. "I've got plenty of fire. And how about you? What have you been up to since you retired? Do you like retirement?"

"I've made all the money I care to make. The fire has well and truly left me." He chuckled to himself. "Anyway, it's nice to be able to travel or relax. Do whatever we like. Margaret does a lot of gardening and takes art classes. We like to go bushwalking together, trying to keep ourselves in shape."

"That sounds lovely."

Lunch was ready then, and they all made their way to the long, polished dining table in the formal dining room. It could seat twenty-four, so they all sat at one end. There was more than enough food to go around—lobster tails, enormous prawns cooked in garlic butter, scallops, and pieces of fish along with roast pork, crackling bread rolls and several different salads.

Sam ate quickly and then left with Meg to find the dogs who'd been locked away before lunch.

"He loves dogs," Maree said. "They won't bite, will they?"

"No, they're sweet little things. But we had to put them away or they'd eat the lobster right out of your hand at the table. They don't have very good manners, I'm afraid. I've coddled them too much," Margaret said.

"Tom tells me you're spending a lot of time together now that he's retired. That must be nice."

Margaret nodded. "We're having the best time. Honestly, we should've done this five years ago. And now that Sam's in our lives, we're hoping he'll get to spend some time here as well. Give you a bit of a break when you need it."

"That will be a big help," Maree said, although she still struggled with the idea of letting go of the control she'd held for the past almost five years. "It might take a while for him to be ready. But we'll play it by ear."

"Of course. We'll come to you, whatever works best. We're just happy to be able to get to know him and to see you again. We've missed you so much." Margaret's eyes glistened with unshed tears. Her words sounded genuine, and it touched Maree to hear them.

"Thank you. I missed you as well. I'm hoping we can all put the past behind us and move forward."

"I'd like that," Margaret said.

Jack rested a hand on Maree's arm. "Thank you," he whispered.

She nodded. "We're family. Right?"

"Family," he agreed.

"And families forgive one another."

"We don't deserve you."

"And don't you forget it," she quipped with a grin.

* * *

After lunch, they found Sam playing with the dogs and coaxed him into the sunroom where the Christmas tree was located with the offer of gifts.

Sam raced into the room and stopped short at the sight of all the gifts beneath the tree. A small black bicycle with training wheels stood in front of it all with a red ribbon attached to the handlebars.

"Santa came!" Sam shouted and ran to the bike, feeling it all over with his little hands.

Maree looked at Jack. "I couldn't help myself."

She wanted to be angry, put out that he'd taken the gift she wanted to give to Sam and gifted it himself. But Sam was also his son. And it was hard to stay angry at Jack for anything, but certainly not for being generous. If she could make Sam happy, she would do almost anything to ensure that happened.

"Thank you," she said.

With a nod, he hurried to help Sam onto the bike. The boy immediately began to pedal, but Jack stopped him. "Whoa, buddy. Let's take it outside after you've opened the rest of your gifts."

Sam agreed and leapt from the bike, rushing over to the tree to squat in front of the pile. He was over the moon to discover that most of the gifts were for him—some from

Santa, others from his new father, grandparents, and aunt. Every time he opened a gift, he squealed with delight and tossed the wrapping paper over his shoulder.

By the time he was done, everyone was exhausted. They'd all received gifts. Maree opened a new blender from Jack—he must've noticed that hers was broken when he was in the flat the last time. His parents gave her a gold necklace with a locket that had space for a photograph. And his sister gave her a massage gift certificate.

"Thank you, everyone," Maree said. "I'm sorry, but I only brought biscuits for all of you. I should've known you'd be so generous."

She felt guilty about not bringing individual presents for each of them. But the homemade biscuits had been all she could manage, and she was proud of how they'd turned out. Sam had helped her pipe green and red icing around the edges, and they'd given tins of them to their neighbours and friends as well.

"Not at all," Margaret said. "You put a lot of effort and thought into that gift. And I am going to love eating them with a cup of tea later."

As the afternoon wore on, they all made their way down to the private beach for a swim. Maree watched Jack and his family build sandcastles, chat, laugh, and play with Sam. She joined in for most of the fun, but at times she liked to stand back and observe. It was a beautiful day. She couldn't have asked for a better one.

Sam was ready to fall to sleep as soon as they were done, so she showered him and dressed him in his pjs for the drive back home.

"Thank you so much for having us," she said.

They all embraced her and thanked her for coming. Finally, she carried her tired boy out to the truck. Jack helped her buckle him in, then they drove home in silence. After Sam was tucked into bed, Jack stood in the living room of the small apartment to talk to her.

"I had a lovely time. Thanks for inviting me," she said.

He nodded. "I'm really glad you came. It was the best Christmas I've had in ... well, years."

"Me too."

He leaned down to kiss her cheek, and then walked to the door.He turned back to smile at her. "We have a pretty great son."

"Yes, we do." Her gaze rested on his. His eyes were intense, full of longing. It caused emotions to well up inside that she wasn't ready to face yet. He seemed to want to go to her, but hesitated, then rested his hand on the door and turned to leave with a shake of his head.

Her heart swelled as he walked out. She'd been alone for so long, she almost couldn't remember what it was like to have someone to share things with. For the first time in a long time, she wasn't alone. They shared a son, and they'd have that in common for the rest of their lives. It felt good to have that connection. To be able to share the joy she felt when he smiled, or the laughter over something sweet that he said, with someone else. It was the best Christmas gift she could've asked for.

Chapter Thirty

Christmas Eve was a quiet affair. Jemma and Dan had gone to her parents for a late-afternoon tea. They didn't much like to entertain, so it was a brief and fairly mundane visit, and they left soon after they'd finished their coffees. As they waved goodbye and pulled out of the driveway, Jemma sighed with relief.

"Done for another year."

"I'm sorry you have such a hard time with them," Dan said.

She shook her head. "I feel really bad about it. They're my parents. I should love them and want to spend time with them. I *do* love them, really. It's just they're so difficult to…"

"Engage in conversation?" Dan quirked an eyebrow at her as he drove.

She laughed. "Yes. What is that about?"

"They really struggle to talk to us about anything at all. When we first got married, I thought they hated me or something. But I soon realised they do the same thing with you. It's as though they have better things to think about than us. I don't know."

She had to admit he was right, even though it pained her to say so. "I didn't notice it so much when I was a kid. I thought it was normal. But they seemed to be waiting for us to leave so they can finally relax and have some fun."

"Well, we don't have to go back again for a while. And there's nothing much to do at home. We didn't cook anything since we thought we'd be eating dinner with them. I still think it's funny they didn't make anything and assumed we'd just be leaving after our coffees."

"I can't understand them," Jemma said with a wave of one hand. "They're my parents, and I don't get it."

"So, we either order takeaway, or go out … or starve."

"Those are our options?" She laughed. "I definitely can't starve."

"Takeaway?"

She nodded. "That sounds perfect. What are you thinking?"

"I'd love some Red Rooster. Those chips with gravy are all I can think about right now."

"I've been craving chips with gravy every single day of my pregnancy, but I've been avoiding them. I don't want to gain too much weight. It's so hard to lose."

"I think we can splash out for Christmas Eve." He turned toward the main street of town.

They picked up dinner and then headed home. It felt good to be in their cozy little unit with delicious food and everything mended between them. They set the food up on the coffee table, poured drinks, and then snuggled together to watch another Christmas movie. It was one of Jemma's favourite Christmas traditions—Christmas movies, good food and quality time together. Besides, lately she fell asleep so early in the evening that going out wasn't something she could really manage.

After dinner, she sat up and stretched her neck to work

out the kinks and then padded to the kitchen to make them both hot chocolate. She'd been loving those lately, even if the weather outside was humid. Inside, they had the air-conditioning cranking, and it was a lovely cool evening.

"Aren't you glad we found this unit when we did?" she said as she returned to the living room with the drinks.

"Hmm."

"Because everything around here is so much more expensive now, and we're still on the contracted rental agreement."

He nodded. "Very glad. It'll help while you're on maternity leave."

"I'd love to buy something as soon as we can manage it."

"I'm working on it, honey."

She didn't want to add more pressure to him. "Don't worry too much about it. It'll happen when we're ready. Maybe after I come back to work, we can focus on saving a deposit."

"That's a good idea."

"In the meantime, if something comes across your desk that looks perfect for us, we should at least talk about it."

"Okay, we can do that." He smiled and patted the couch. "Come on—let's finish this movie. Then we should go to bed or Santa won't come."

She laughed as she sat next to him. "But you've been a bad boy. I don't know if he's coming anyway."

He lunged for her, and she squealed, jumping out of the way and almost spilling the drinks. He chased her into the bedroom, her laughter leading the way.

Chapter Thirty-One

Sam woke impossibly early. The sun wasn't up yet, and he was already bouncing beside Maree's bed. Her eyes blinked open, and she tried to focus on his sweet face, but it was a blur. She rubbed them and tried again.

"Merry Christmas, buddy," she rasped. "You're awake a little early. Do you think you could go back to bed and have a few more minutes of sleep?"

"No way! Come on, Mum! Santa came again! He came yesterday and today. Twice!"

His golden hair flopped on his head with every jump. She couldn't help smiling. "Okay, I'm coming. Just give me a minute to find some toothpicks to prop my eyes open."

Within ten minutes, she was wrapped in her robe, coffee mug in hand, seated on the couch with her legs tucked up beneath her. Sam was excitedly pushing each of his gifts into a semi-neat pile while he waited for Jack, who Maree had texted as soon as she could get her eyes to focus.

Jack walked in with a smile on his face. "Merry Christmas!"

"Merry Christmas," Maree whispered, holding a finger to

her lips. "Jemma and Dan are still sleeping. They don't wake easily, thank goodness. But we should probably try to be quiet."

"That might be difficult," Jack said with a laugh as Sam ran over and launched himself at his father's legs with a yell, embracing him. It made Maree's heart contract to see them together like this. She cleared her throat and took another sip of coffee.

"Did you sleep well?" she asked as he took a seat beside her.

"I did, thanks. What a lovely day."

She groaned. "Is it? I'm not sure I'm awake enough to know where I am, and you're sounding impossibly chipper."

He laughed. "I see nothing has changed."

"I'm never going to be a morning person. It's just a reality we should all accept."

Sam was so excited when they said he could open his gifts. One by one, he tore off the wrapping paper. Then, after he was done, he disappeared into his bedroom with the bulldozer Maree had bought him, leaving them alone.

"That went well," Jack said.

"I love Christmas through his eyes."

"It's pretty special from where I'm sitting, too."

His words warmed her heart. He was right. There was something very special about what they had now with Jack back in their lives. She'd felt alone for so long. Heartbroken over losing her best friend, soulmate and husband. Could she give him another chance?

"I have a gift for you." He pulled a small present wrapped in gold paper out of his pocket and handed it to her.

"Another one? You didn't have to do that. I'm sorry—I didn't have much for you. Just the biscuits."

"I love your biscuits." He winked.

She laughed. "I'm glad to hear it." She unwrapped the gift

and found a simple gold ring with a sapphire in the setting. It was beautiful, classic. And it looked very much like an engagement band.

"Jack..."

He leaned in close, placed a hand on either side of her face, and stared into her eyes. "Tell me you feel it too."

She inhaled a jagged breath. "I do, but..."

"Don't question—just go with it. We've had so much thrown our way. We've been through more than any young married couple should. But this is our opportunity to start again. To try to make amends for everything that's happened. I want us to give our marriage another go. What do you think?"

She stared into his grey eyes and couldn't come up with a single reason why not. "I think ... I think you're the love of my life. I think ... I can't imagine living without you and every second apart has broken me into pieces. I don't know if I trust you to stay, but I know I can't turn you away."

Tears glimmered in the corners of his eyes. "I promise I won't hurt you again. I'll be here, every day, for the rest of our lives."

He smiled widely, then leaned down to kiss her on the lips. His were soft and yet determined. She drew closer to him, leaning against his firm body as the pain, loneliness and sorrow of the last five years melted away.

Chapter Thirty-Two

The sun shone down on a bright Christmas Day on Sunshine Beach. The waves curled to shore, sparkling beneath the glare. The sand was hot on her feet, and Jemma grimaced as she hurried back up to the covered BBQ area beneath a row of hoop pines.

"Sand's hot!" she called.

Dan's family stood around the BBQ while his brother turned the meat over, one piece at a time. His mother was down at the water's edge with her daughter-in-law and grandchildren. His father hovered by his brother's elbow, pointing at sausages and saying things like "That one's ready."

She smiled at Dan and reached for a bottle of lemonade, pouring herself a cup before taking a deep drink. She was thirsty. And hungry. Lunch was a little late, so she'd been snacking on chips and fruit. But her stomach was growling again. She'd have to eat soon.

Dan came over to see her. "Are you going to have a swim?"

"Maybe later. I'm starving. Is lunch almost ready? Do you need a hand with anything?"

"I think it's just about done. Brett won't let me touch the

meat, but I sliced the tomatoes. Didn't I do a good job?" He held up a tray of sliced tomatoes with a proud smile.

She laughed. "Wow. Incredible, really. I don't know how you did that so well."

"While we're alone, I wanted to give you something. We didn't get a chance to do gifts this morning since we slept in."

"I have no idea how you slept through the noise of Sam opening his gifts and pushing his new bulldozer around the house."

He grunted. "I didn't hear a thing."

"Lucky you. I put earplugs in and drifted back off to sleep, thankfully. I was exhausted."

"Well, anyway," he continued, "I wanted to give you my gift while no one else was around." He pulled a box out from beneath the picnic table. It was wrapped in pink Christmas paper with a large gold ribbon tied into a bow in the centre.

"Wow, it's huge. How did you sneak that out of the car without me seeing it?"

"I have magical powers. Open it."

He set it on the table next to her, and she pulled the wrapping off carefully, not wanting to tear it too badly. She loved to reuse beautiful paper for the various crafts she did in her downtime.

Inside was a large box with the word "bouncer" printed on it, along with a picture of a baby.

"It rocks the baby from side to side. They can sleep in this thing. Apparently, it's amazing. The guy at the store said we'll never want to go without it."

She grinned. "That's so sweet. Thank you. Very thoughtful."

"And I got you this as well," he added, handing her a small box. This one was wrapped with blue paper and another gold ribbon.

She opened it and found a long, gold necklace with a figurine of a mother cradling a baby in her arms strung onto the chain,. "It's beautiful, Dan. Wow, I love it."

"I thought it could remind you of how much I'm looking forward to spending my life with you and the baby, as a family."

Her throat tightened, and she threw her arms around his neck. "I'll think of you every time I look at it."

Chapter Thirty-Three

Maree held on to the cricket bat and tapped the end of it against the sand. She squinted into the sunlight. It was Boxing Day, the day after Christmas, and she was on Sunshine Beach with a group of friends playing beach cricket. Christmas was over, but the celebrations had continued into the next day. She felt relaxed and happy for the first time in a long time.

She and Jack had reunited. She could hardly believe it was real. Every time she looked at him, standing with his hands on his hips, waiting for her to hit the ball so he might catch her out, she couldn't help grinning.

"Come on, honey, you're dragging this out," Jack said with a wink as he braced himself with his feet apart.

The bowl came slow and steady from Mark. His arm straight, he levelled the throw so it wouldn't bounce on the sand but would come straight to Maree. Any bounce on the sand would send the ball careening off in the wrong direction. And with the soft balls they were using, a bowl could easily be slowed down enough for every one of them, no matter how skilled, to have a chance at a hit.

Maree raised the bat and swung for the ball. It connected,

and the ball sailed over his head. Gwen reached for it but missed. She had to scramble after it through the sand. She tripped and fell into Joanna, who stumbled backward laughing. The two of them landed in a heap, arms and legs flailing.

"Are you okay?" Chris called out. He was Joanna's neighbour, and newly minted boyfriend, from what Maree could tell. The two of them were very cute together. She'd always liked Joanna, who'd been a chef at the best restaurant on the island when Maree was little.

"We're fine," Joanna replied, still laughing.

She and Gwen got to their feet while Maree jogged back and forth, chalking up runs as best she could in the hot sand.

"I'm going to get heat stroke," she complained. "Can we go for a swim now?"

Everyone agreed that would be the best course of action and headed for the waves. At the shoreline, Maree stripped off her summer dress. Her red bikini was new, and she was glad she'd taken the time to go shopping after last Christmas during the sales. Her previous swimsuit was practically falling apart.

Jack reached for her, pulling her close. Sam played nearby, digging in the sand. Debbie Holmes and her husband sat with him, piling wet sand on top of a huge structure they'd been building for the past half an hour.

Jack's hands slid around her waist. She spun to face him, looping her hands around his neck, smiling up at him.

"Hello, Mr. Houston."

"Hello, Mrs. Houston."

"We're not married yet."

"But you never changed your name ... I wondered if that meant you still had hope for a future together." He tipped his head to one side to study her, his mouth curled into a half grin.

"I always had hope. But I wouldn't admit it, even to myself."

"Are you happy?" he asked.

She spun free of his grasp and ran into the waves, giggling and squealing as the cold water splashed against her. She dove beneath a wave with Jack close behind. He tackled her beyond the break, and they tumbled under the water together, arms and legs tangled up in a mess of limbs.

When her head broke through the surface, she gasped for air, still laughing. He came up beside her, shaking the water from his hair before swimming closer to encircle her once again in his arms. It felt right to bob there, beyond the break, in the cool blue water. The sun glanced off the ocean's surface, and fish danced about their feet.

"I'm very happy," she said finally.

And when he kissed her, the entire world stood still. It was a moment of pure joy. Of contentment and hope for a better future. Her family was whole. And she would do everything she could never to let it fracture again.

Epilogue

Five months later, it was May, and the weather had cooled. Jemma's stomach felt enormous. She imagined that every step she took made her look more and more like a waddling duck. None of her clothes fit, so she'd had to visit the maternity section at the mall and thankfully had managed to find a pair of elastic-waisted jeans. That, coupled with some shirts, was getting her through most days, although she hated dressing down all the time after working in real estate for years.

"What should we do today?" she asked.

Dan was reading a mountain biking magazine on the couch. It was his first day off work all week, and Jemma was determined they'd do something enjoyable together. He'd been working so hard, and since the nausea of her early pregnancy passed, she'd been working almost as hard to get their business into shape for her maternity leave. They were both finally satisfied that Dan could keep things going without Jemma in the office, at least for the next six to twelve months. They'd have to play it by ear. Thankfully, the business was theirs, so they could manage it the way they thought best.

"I don't feel like doing anything much," Dan said with a yawn. "I'm tired."

"I know, but it might be a while before we can get out of the house, just the two of us. The baby is due any day now. In fact, she was due a week ago. And I feel like I'm expanding by the minute. Surely she won't keep me waiting much longer."

He smiled. "I'm sorry, honey. I wish there was something we could do about it. Isn't walking supposed to help?"

Jemma sighed. "I don't feel like walking. My hips are doing something wonky. It's like they're out of alignment. And I'm so breathless."

"It could help you get into labour, though. So, maybe we should give it a try?"

He was right. She knew they should take a walk. She only wished there was something else that would work, like maybe a romantic dinner at her favourite restaurant or a swim.

"Should we take a swim after in the heated pool?"

"Absolutely. That sounds perfect," Dan replied.

Jemma changed into a long dress and donned a large straw hat. Then the two of them headed out to the beach. The sun had dipped towards the horizon, and long shadows stretched down the beach. She shivered as the wind picked up, whipping at her dress.

"I should've worn the jeans," she said, one hand holding her dress in place, the other holding onto her hat.

"Let me have the hat. Come on, we'll head back. I think we've gone far enough."

She was breathing hard and they'd barely made it a few houses down from their own apartment complex, but she was already spent.

"Okay, thanks. This sand is hard to walk in, and I'm so heavy."

"You've got to take care of yourself."

A stabbing cramp reverberated through her abdomen. "Whoa."

"What is it?" Dan stopped, looking concerned.

"I felt something."

"Labour?"

"Maybe. I don't know."

"We've got to get you back up to the footpath." His eyes were wide and he held on to her elbow, guiding her up the sandy beach and along the path through the dunes.

The pain came again. This time it was more intense and lasted longer.

"Oh, ouch. Yes, I think it might be labour." She grimaced. "Hurry. I'm not having this baby on the beach."

They made it back home, and Jemma called the hospital to tell them what was going on. They assured her she had plenty of time and that she should find a way to relax. She decided to take a shower, and it did help to relax her. After a while, the pains were closer together, and they drove to the hospital.

It took sixteen hours, but finally their little pink bundle of joy arrived. They called her Katherine Anna, and she was delightful, with a thick head of black hair that fell across her forehead.

Dan stood beside the bassinet looking down at the baby with a proud expression on his handsome face. She was sleeping soundly on her back, wrapped neatly in a pink floral baby blanket.

"She's beautiful," he whispered.

"She's absolutely perfect," Jemma agreed, her throat tightening. She'd been very emotional since Katherine arrived. She found it hard to believe that cute little creature was theirs. That the baby she'd so longed for had finally arrived, and their lives would never be the same again.

"Can we do this?" Dan glanced over at her, his forehead creased. "She's so small."

Jemma gave him a lopsided grin. "We can do it. It's going to be great."

"You're always so confident and positive."

"Because I know you, and you're going to be a wonderful father. I've wanted to be a mother for so long. It's going to be hard, but I also believe we can handle this. It's everything we've been hoping for. She's here and she's healthy and gorgeous. What else could we want out of life?"

He laughed. "You're right. I feel completely satisfied and utterly scared at the same time."

"We'll figure it out. Other people do this every day. If they can do it, so can we."

He walked over to her bed and took her hand. She lay beneath the white sheets, her entire body somewhere between exhausted and exhilarated. He raised her hand to his lips and kissed the back of it.

"We're a family. From this point on, no more pushing each other away. Deal?"

She nodded. "It's us against the world. Til death..."

He grinned. "Now we just have to figure out how to get her home in that car seat."

* * *

*Thank you for reading **A Sunshine Christmas**! I hope you enjoyed visiting Sunshine, Bribie Island.*

Next, dive into The Honeysuckle Cafe...

Matilda travels to the land of peaches, honeysuckle and grits to discover her roots, and along the way unwinds the secrets and lies that have followed her throughout all the twists and turns of life.

"**Love, love, love** these books!" ☆☆☆☆☆

Want to find out about all of my new releases? Click here to be notified about new stories when you download this free book!

Keep scrolling to find out about all of my other books.

If you'd like to join my exclusive Facebook reader group, where we talk about what we're reading and have other fun together, you can do that here.

WOMEN'S FICTION

THE SUNSHINE SERIES

The Sunshine Potluck Society
Four friends start a monthly potluck brunch when their lives begin to unravel.
Sunshine Reservations
An old bed and breakfast by the beach and a restaurant that was burned to the ground, give Gwen an opportunity to start afresh after divorce.
The Summer Pact
When Beth Prince was thirteen years old she met a boy on New Year's Eve at Sunshine Beach. They talked all night and when the sun rose they vowed that they'd meet back at the same place in 15 years.
A Sunshine Christmas
Maree Houston's ex-husband is back in Sunshine for

Christmas and she quickly discovers that a stolen kiss could ruin everything. Including her big secret.

CORAL ISLAND SERIES

The Island

After twenty five years of marriage and decades caring for her two children, on the evening of their vow renewal, her husband shocks her with the news that he's leaving her.

The Beach Cottage

Beatrice is speechless. It's something she never expected — a secret daughter. She and Aidan have only just renewed their romance, after decades apart, and he never mentioned a child. Did he know she existed?

The Blue Shoal Inn

Taya's inn is in trouble. Her father has built a fancy new resort in Blue Shoal and hired a handsome stranger to manage it. When the stranger offers to buy her inn and merge it with the resort, she wants to hate him but when he rescues a stray dog her feelings for him change.

Island Weddings

Charmaine moves to Coral Island and lands a job working at a local florist shop. It seems as though the entire island has caught wedding fever, with weddings planned every weekend. It's a good opportunity for her to get to know the locals, but what she doesn't expect is to be thrown into the middle of a family drama.

The Island Bookshop

Evie's book club friends are the people in the world she relies on most. But when one of the newer members finds herself confronted with her past, the rest of the club will do what they can to help, endangering the existence of the bookshop without realising it.

An Island Reunion

HISTORICAL FICTION (WRITING AS BRONWEN PRATLEY)

Beyond the Crushing Waves

An emotional standalone historical saga. Two children plucked from poverty & forcibly deported from the UK to Australia. Inspired by true events. An unforgettable tale of loss, love, redemption & new beginnings.

Under a Sunburnt Sky

Inspired by a true story. Jan Kostanski is a normal Catholic boy in Warsaw when the nazis invade. He's separated from his neighbours, a Jewish family who he considers kin, by the ghetto wall. Jan and his mother decide that they will do whatever it takes to save their Jewish friends from certain death. The unforgettable tale of an everyday family's fight against evil, and the unbreakable bonds of their love.

About the Author

Lilly Mirren is an Amazon top 20, Audible top 15 and *USA Today* Bestselling author who has sold over two million copies of her books worldwide. She lives in Brisbane, Australia with her husband and three children.

Her books combine heartwarming storylines with realistic characters readers see as friends.

Her debut series, *The Waratah Inn*, set in the delightful Cabarita Beach, hit the *USA Today* Bestseller list and since then, has touched the hearts of hundreds of thousands of readers across the globe.